the first RULE

INTERNATIONAL BESTSELLING AUTHOR
NICOLE S. GOODIN

THE FIRST RULE

NICOLE S. GOODIN

Paperback Edition
ISBN: 978-0-473-58512-9

The First Rule
First published August 2021
All rights reserved. ©
Cover design by Nicole Goodin
Images purchased from Deposit Photos
Editing by Spell Bound

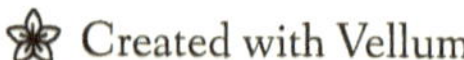 Created with Vellum

DISCLAIMER

This book is a work of fiction. All names, characters, places and incidents either are products of the author's imagination or are used fictitiously. Any resemblance to events, places, or persons, living or dead, is purely coincidental.

The author acknowledges all song titles, song lyrics, film titles, film characters, trademarked statuses and brands mentioned in this book are the property of, and belong to, their respective owners.

Nicole S. Goodin is in no way affiliated with any of the brands, songs, musicians or artists mentioned in this book.

To everyone who makes someone smile like they've never smiled before.

AUTHOR'S NOTE

This book has been written using UK English and may contain euphemisms and slang words that form part of the New Zealand spoken word.
Please remember that the words are not misspelled. They are slang terms and form part of everyday, New Zealand vernacular.
I.e: I'm from New Zealand and sometimes we say weird things down here... please try and be cool about it.

PROLOGUE

Darcy

"I can't do this anymore."

Five words you don't want to hear on your wedding day from the man you thought you'd spend the rest of your life with.

A living nightmare.

Every bride's worst fear.

My reality.

ONE

Darcy

"I don't want to see anyone!" I scream at the locked door of the hotel's honeymoon suite.

I know that Freya and Steph are just trying to be there for me, I *do*, but I can't even look either of them in the eye right now, I'm mortified... *humiliated...* heartbroken.

It's been – I check the time on the huge clock on the wall – *three* hours since the man who got down on one knee and proposed to me ten months ago, shattered my life into a million pieces.

The longest three hours of my life.

I down another shot, just for good measure.

The pounding on the door continues. "Open up, Darcy, *right now.*"

The voice isn't any of the ones I'm expecting, and for a moment my heart races in my chest, because that voice is familiar, it's *his* voice. I creep towards the door, pressing my palms against the white panels, hope swelling stupidly in my chest.

"It's Ryan, open up or so help me God, I'll knock the door down."

Tears spring to my eyes.

It's *Ryan*. Not Jacob.

Ryan – my fiancé's twin brother. *Ex-fiancé* I should say, because I know damn well that when Jacob walked down that aisle, *away* from me, that it wasn't just an 'I'm not ready for marriage' moment, it was a 'we're over' one.

I let my forehead fall forward, so it's resting on the door. He starts banging on the other side again and my head pounds with each thump.

"Go away, Ryan," I finally say.

It's not loud, and it's not firm, but he hears me. The pounding stops.

"*Darcy.*" My name is a plea. "Please, Darcy, just let me in."

"I *can't*," I say, my voice cracking as tears stream down my cheeks for the millionth time.

"Sure you can, just turn the lock, and I'll do the rest."

"Just let me get drunk in peace," I beg.

"Not until you let me in."

Ryan and Jacob are the two most identical twins I've ever seen in my entire life. They're eerily similar, to the point where their own father is unable to tell them apart the majority of the time – at least that was the case until Ryan went away for a few months about four and a half years ago and came back sporting a rather large collection of piercings and tattoos, a new hair style and a brand new attitude.

But even given the cosmetic differences between the two men, their eyes are still the exact same shade of green, and the thought of having to look into Ryan's eyes – *Jacob's eyes* – right now, scares the shit out of me.

I don't reply, and the silence rings in my ears.

"I'm not *him*, Darcy... *please*, let me in..." He's silent for a few beats. "I know how to drink..."

I huff out a laugh, but it gets caught in my throat by my unshed tears.

I know he's not Jacob, but being stubborn is a trait both men possess, so I also know he won't leave until I open this door.

"I'm not going anywhere until I see you," he says, his words mirroring my thoughts, "so you may as well just open up. I'll wait out here as long as it takes."

I sigh, resigned.

The absolute last thing I want right now is anybody bearing witness to any more of my humilia-tion, but after today, I don't expect to ever see anyone from Jacob's family again, so I guess it doesn't really matter if Ryan views me in all my hot mess glory. He's just become somebody that I used to know.

It's not like Ryan and I were ever close anyway,

he and Jacob "grew apart", that's what Jacob always said, so if he sees me at my worst possible moment, I doubt that will be the thing keeping me awake at night. I've got much bigger problems in the scheme of things.

I reach my hand towards the lock, my fingers lingering on the cool metal for a moment before turning over the bolt to allow him access to the suite.

The door pushes inwards immediately, but slowly... tentatively, as though he's unsure of exactly what he might walk in on.

"Don't worry, I didn't go all *The Hangover* and smash up the place," I say humourlessly. "There's no tiger in the bathroom."

"Wouldn't blame you if you did."

His voice is calm, soft... *understanding*. It's not pitying like I expected it to be, and I couldn't be more grateful. Pity has never been something I appreciated, and I can't imagine that changing at this point in time.

I suck in a brave, shallow breath and allow myself to meet the green eyes that I know will be trained on my face.

Ryan and I might not be close, but one thing I've learnt about him over the five years since I've been with Jacob, is that he *always* looks directly into my eyes when he talks to me. It's unnerving and, frankly, a little odd, it's almost as though he's willing me to look back into his – to find *something* there.

Sure enough, those bright eyes are boring holes

into mine with all the intensity of a thousand suns. He breathes out harshly and releases me from his hold as he steps across the threshold.

"Why are you here?" I allow myself to look him over, focusing only on the differences between the two men, and ignoring the similarities.

He shuts the door behind himself and rests his back against it, mirroring my position on the door at my side.

"I was thirsty," he replies dryly, a slight smirk pulling at the corner of his mouth, his lip piercing sticking out slightly with the movement.

Laughter bubbles up my chest and out of my mouth, surprising both of us. I laugh long and hard as he watches me curiously, likely trying to figure out if I've lost my mind.

I must be quite the sight, still in my elaborate, insanely expensive white wedding dress, my veil hanging haphazardly from my once flawless up-do.

This dress cost thousands of dollars, the shoes have some ridiculous price tag too, and I'll be donating them both to a charity store at the earliest possible convenience. I never want to see a shred of evidence of this day ever again.

My laugh dies off at the sobering reminder of the mess my life is in.

"I'm here," Ryan says softly, sensing the change in my demeanour.

It's an obvious statement, but one that I didn't know I needed to hear.

I'm so alone.

I sent away my friends... I don't have any family anymore, and now I don't have Jacob either, but for right now at least, I *do* have Ryan.

I take a real, deep breath for what feels like the first time since my husband-to-be ran out on me.

"Are you okay?" he asks, his tone cautious.

I shake my head. "You'd have more reason to be concerned if I *was* okay. Don't you think?"

He nods his head in silent agreement.

We fall into the quiet again, letting it surround us. My thoughts wander back to the moment that I'm still not convinced wasn't just all some bad dream.

"Did you know he was going to do it?" I ask, already knowing the answer, but unable to force the question to go away unasked either.

"No." His answer is swift, undoubtedly truthful. I know this not only because he and Jacob haven't been close enough to be confidants in a long time, but because I know Ryan can't look me in the eye and lie to me. It's not in his nature.

He's not like his brother, who apparently has absolutely no issue lying to my face whatsoever, and has been for god only knows how long at this point.

I dread to think what else he might have lied to me about over the years.

I nod slowly, his answer doing nothing to satisfy my need to know what the hell happened to cause my life to implode around me without notice.

"He's a prick, Darcy. Don't try and find any

explanation other than that. You could spend the rest of your life trying to find a way to justify what he just did to you, but you won't find one. There's no excuse for it. *None.*"

I nod again.

I can feel the tequila really starting to take hold of my inhibitions. I'm getting that all over fuzzy feeling. It's nice, but it's not enough.

Numb. I need to feel numb, fuzzy isn't going to cut it right now.

I push off the door, hiking up my dress as I cross the huge room towards the bottle of golden liquid.

"You coming?" I prompt when I hear nothing behind me.

His footsteps follow, the soft pad a stark contrast to the heavy-footed ones of his brother that I've grown so used to over the years.

I shake my head. I have to stop doing that. Stop thinking about Jacob. Stop thinking at all. Just *stop.*

I reach for the bottle and bring it up to my lips, but Ryan's tattooed arm snakes out, his hand taking the bottle from me before I can make contact with the top.

"I think a glass would be smart."

"Maybe I don't want to be smart."

He lowers the bottle, both of us still holding it as we make eye contact again.

It strikes me then, as the alcohol settles further into my veins, just how striking Ryan really is. Sure, he's identical to Jacob, but the bad-boy air that surrounds him suits him so well. The piercings, the tattoos, the scruff on his jaw... the bike... it just *works*.

"Why'd you do it?" The question is out of my mouth before I can stop it.

Tequila courage.

I've always wondered what happened all those years ago that caused him to quit the family business and go rogue.

When I met Jacob, and then Ryan shortly after, both men had been clean-cut businessmen. Short back and sides haircut, no facial hair. Ink-free skin. Jacob is still the same now as he was then – right down to the same haircut, but *Ryan*... Ryan couldn't be less like the man I first met.

FOUR AND A HALF YEARS AGO:

"IS RYAN COMING TONIGHT?"

Jacob doesn't hear me, he's got his nose in his tablet, probably looking at the stock market or tallying shares or something else I don't really understand.

"Jake?" I try again.

He hears me this time, glancing in my direction. "What's that?"

"Is Ryan coming tonight?" I repeat. "Your dad said he was back in town..."

"Don't know, don't care."

"You should care; he's your only brother."

I'd give anything for even another ten minutes with my family, so I've never been able to understand the void between Jacob and Ryan.

He shrugs, his attention back on his tablet.

"It's your dad's sixtieth birthday."

He doesn't even answer me.

I'm about to push Jacob on it again when I see him. Ryan. Only he looks nothing like the Ryan I last saw.

His hair is longer on top, his face covered in masculine scruff, but not only that, he's covered in tattoos, and there is a glimmer of silver through his lip and eyebrow.

He meets my eyes instantly, as though he knew exactly where to find me, waiting.

Emotion swims in those green pools, and I gasp.

"Guess he came after all," I hear Jacob sneer from next to me.

"DO *WHAT*?" Ryan asks, interrupting my daydream.

I shake my head in a feeble attempt to clear my thoughts.

"The tattoos... the piercings."

My gaze drifts from his eyes to the ring in his left eyebrow. He has metal in both his lip and his brow still, and I'm suddenly curious to know if anything else on his body bears more of the same.

He shrugs a shoulder. "Why not?"

"Just seems like a drastic change."

He gently pulls the bottle from my grasp and turns away from me, pouring the liquid into two crystal glasses. "I decided I wanted to be my own man, not one half of a pair."

He mutters his reply quietly, but I hear it.

"Huh," I muse aloud. I've never thought about it like that.

He really was one half of a pair. Identical in virtually every sense of the word. Career, appearance, mannerisms, style, voice... I couldn't exactly blame him for wanting to carve his own path.

He turns, his arm extended to offer me a glass. I take it from him, and he moves towards the bed, sitting down on the edge. He's still wearing his suit pants, but he's ditched his jacket, and the sleeves of his crisp white shirt are rolled up to reveal his forearms.

"You could have just grown a beard and got a new haircut... you didn't have to walk away from the future you worked so hard for."

He raises a dark brow at me. "I didn't come in here to talk about me."

"Humour me," I insist. "*Please.*"

I'd give just about anything for a distraction from my life – even just for ten minutes.

His eyes rake over me, starting at my messed-up hair and trailing all the way down to my bare feet.

"Did you ever consider that it wasn't the future I

wanted? That I'm nothing like my father or my brother?"

I contemplate that as I cross the room to sit on the other side of the huge bed.

I sip at my drink. I really must be getting drunk, because I don't even wince as it burns its way down my throat.

"You don't want your share of the billion-dollar Steele business?"

He studies me, the emotion in his bright eyes unreadable.

"Money doesn't buy happiness, Darce."

Don't I know it.

I slug back the rest of the contents from the glass in my hand.

"Easy now. You're not much of a drinker," he warns.

"How would you know what I am?" I fire at him, the question coming out far surlier than intended, even though he's bang on the money with his comment somehow. I'm *not* much of a drinker.

If he notices my tone, he doesn't react. Instead, he sips his own drink and continues watching me.

I pull my eyes away, unable to handle the intense scrutiny he's putting me under. My gaze lands on my discarded heels, and right next to them, hundreds of dollars of flowers that made up my bouquet, which is now shredded entirely to pieces.

I feel my frustrations building – with Ryan a little

bit, with myself perhaps... I'm not entirely sure, but *definitely* with Jacob.

"Let it out, Darce."

My eyes snap back to Ryan's, my mind racing, confused about his ability to somehow read me like a book – this man who doesn't really know me at all.

"You don't want me to let it out," I reply bitterly.

"Let. It. Out." Each word is enunciated, clear... concise.

I snap, throwing the glass across the room where it hits the wall and smashes into a thousand pieces. "How could he do this to me?" I scream. "This isn't some shitty Hollywood movie where the groom runs out on the bride, this is my life, my *fucking* life!"

Ryan just sits there, calmly watching me, willing me to continue.

I climb off the bed, my ridiculous dress nearly tripping me.

I claw at it, pulling the lengths of fabric out of my way.

I point at Ryan, my chest heaving. "Who the fuck does that? I gave him five years of my life. I gave him *everything* I had to give."

"I know you did."

The softness in his tone weakens me.

"And he just left me." My voice cracks, tears pooling in my eyes instantly. "Why does everybody I love leave me?"

He's on his feet, standing in front of me in time to catch me as I sag forward, collapsing under the weight of the betrayal, my body racking with heavy sobs as I do what Ryan told me to do, and let it all out. They're not just tears for Jacob, they're tears for everything I've lost.

I sob for what feels like forever, until I'm finally all cried out, and Ryan holds me, his strong arms bearing my weight effortlessly as I drain myself of all emotion.

"We were trying for a baby," I say, my voice rough but quiet.

His posture tenses for a moment before relaxing again.

"You're not... you're not pregnant, are you?"

I shake my head, my body wills me to cry some more, but my eyes refuse to give up any more tears.

"A year we've tried. And *nothing*."

Maybe that's why he walked out – because I'm broken... because there must be something wrong with me. Jacob probably wants a woman who can give him a child, someone to carry on his precious family name and produce him an heir to his throne.

"It's not your fault," Ryan says softly.

"You don't know that. What if it *is* my fault we couldn't have a baby?"

He pulls back, his shoulder soaked from my tears and looks me in the eye. "I'm not a fertility doctor, Darcy, I'm not telling you that there's nothing stopping you from getting pregnant, but I am telling you that it's not your *fault*."

It all sounds so simple when he says it like that.

"I was pregnant once," I say, the words falling from my lips without permission.

The alcohol I've consumed in the past few hours has loosened my tongue dangerously. I never over-share like this. I shouldn't be now either, but something about him makes me want to keep talking.

He doesn't speak but waits for me to go on.

"I was nineteen. I wasn't ready for a baby. I had no money, no support... the father was a drop-kick loser. I had a termination, Ryan. What if I'm being punished for not keeping that baby? What if this is my karma?" My voice has taken on a hysterical edge as I voice aloud all my deepest, darkest fears and secrets.

He pulls me tighter and leads me down onto the bed, his arms still wrapped around me. His hand skimming up and down my back as he shushes me, soothing me.

I feel all my muscles relax as I allow myself to be comforted by him.

He might not be the man I thought I'd be sharing this room with tonight, but he's close, so for now, that'll have to be enough.

My eyelids grow heavier and heavier, the alcohol doing its best to pull me under.

"You'll be a mother, Darce. I promise you," I hear Ryan say as I fight a losing battle against my subconscious. "I'll make sure of it."

TWO

Ryan

Her cheeks are tear-stained and her hair is all messed up, but I swear to God, I've still never seen anyone look so beautiful.

Not even the hell my brother just unleashed on her could dull the shine in those crystal blue eyes. They might be bloodshot and puffy, but they're *alive*.

She's still in there, fighting, pushing through, and if I were a better man, I'd leave with that knowledge – the reassurance that she'll be okay eventually – and let her work through her grief in her own time, but I just *can't*.

I can't walk out of this room while she's sleeping. I can't let another Steele man leave her alone today. Just the thought threatens to crush me.

I glance at her sleeping form again as she exhales deeply.

My brother is a complete and utter fucking moron – not that I wasn't already aware of that fact, but the choice he made this afternoon highlights it now more than ever.

He just gave up the best thing in his *entire* life. She's the only thing he had that really mattered.

Women like Darcy aren't replaceable. She's one of a kind. I should know, I've been trying to find even one that could compare to her for the past five years, and I've come up empty.

Worse than empty even – I've tortured myself over and over again by comparing her to anyone and everyone I've come across.

The only woman that has been a constant in my life, the only woman I can stand to be around, is Rebel – I hate to think what my life might be like if she hadn't shouldered her way in and then refused to leave.

The thought reminds me – she text me earlier, after she heard the shocking news – and I haven't had a chance to reply to her.

I watch Darcy as I carefully slide my phone from my pocket, trying not to jostle her head, which is laid in my lap.

Rebel: DUDE, what the hell?! Never a dull moment in the Steele family. What the fuck happened?

I tap out a reply, unsure of what to say. I can't think of a way to explain this. I don't even know how she's heard, but I shouldn't be surprised; Rebel knows everything about everyone.

Ryan: No idea. I'm with Darcy right now, she's sleeping. She got drunk, angry, cried… I'll see how she is when she wakes up.

Her reply comes quickly, as I knew it would – her phone is practically glued to her hand ninety-eight percent of the time.

Rebel: Bad idea, Ryan.

Ryan: I'm just trying to make it easier for her.

Rebel: By making it harder for yourself?

I scrub my hand over my face as the woman in my lap stirs. Rebel's right. This isn't smart of me. I, of all people, shouldn't be here, and not only because my appearance is bound to make it harder for the very person I'm trying to help, but because I've secretly been in love with Darcy Shearer since the first day I met her.

FIVE YEARS AGO:

.   .   .

"OH C'MON, how hard is it to open a couple of beers? Hell, I'll pay double at this point!" the tiny blonde next to me yells as she glares at the bartender who is favouring the other end of the bar and has been all night.

"I'll give you a leg up and you can get me a couple while you're there," I offer.

She turns around to face me, and my next smart remark gets caught in my throat. She's hands down the most beautiful woman I've ever seen in my whole life.

She raises a brow at me as she looks me up and down, checking out my costume. "If you really were Superman, you'd fly over there and get them for us, you know that, right?"

I shrug. "Maybe I'm just Clark Kent tonight."

She giggles and her blonde hair falls over one of her eyes. She extends her hand to me. "Nice to meet you, Clark, my name's Barbie."

I take her tiny hand in my much bigger one. "The pleasure is all mine, Barbie."

THAT WAS the moment my whole life changed forever. Nothing was the same after that night. No matter how much I tried to force it to go back to the way it was before her, everything shifted in the half-second that it took for our eyes to meet.

Darcy rolls over and the familiar scent of her perfume wafts towards me. She might have changed in a lot of ways in the past five years, but her scent has remained the same. It's not helping me close the door on memory lane in the least.

I watch as her lids slowly flutter open, and her eyes take a moment to focus on my face above her.

"Ryan," she says, her voice thick with sleep, and I know I shouldn't feel the pang of satisfaction that it's my name on her lips and not Jacob's, but I do.

"I'm here," I promise.

She drags her hand over her face, smudging her makeup further. "Part of me was really hoping I'd dreamed that you came and saw me like this."

I know better than to be hurt by her words. There's been a lot of things that have hurt me over the years where Darcy is concerned, but not a single one of those has been her fault, and this isn't about me, it's about *her*. She's humiliated.

My leg twitches, and she glances down. "Shit... sorry," she mutters as the realisation that she's got her head in my lap hits.

"It's okay. I'm glad you got some sleep."

"Why are you here, Ryan? You don't even like me."

She's not wrong. I don't *like* her. I love her.

I hate that she thinks I don't like her, but I did what I had to do all these years. I stayed away. I couldn't just sit by and watch my brother live happily ever after with the woman of *my* dreams. I had to go. I had to push that life away. I had to distance myself.

"I told you, I'm here to drink."

"Fine," she sighs, "but you've got some serious catching up to do."

She does seem more sober than before her nap, but I have no idea how many drinks she downed before I got into the room.

I nod my head as she sits up and leans back against the huge, elaborate gold headboard. I get up and pour us both a drink, a little heavier handed this time – something tells me we're both going to need it. I tuck the bottle under my arm and bring that with me too, if this goes the way I expect it to, it will be empty in no time.

She smiles sadly at me as I pass her drink.

"What a mess, huh?" She shrugs.

I settle in next to her, both of us staring ahead, avoiding looking at one another. "It's not your fault. None of it. My brother is a bastard."

"I'm starting to think you might be right."

I'm definitely right, but it's not really the time for *I told you so's*.

"What happened between you two?" she questions. "You were close once."

You happened, I think to myself. Words that I'll probably never say aloud.

I shake my head, grimacing. "It's complicated."

It's really not complicated at all. In fact, it's so, *so* simple.

Jacob showed his true colours once again, only that particular time, I didn't take it lying down. I stood up for myself, *finally*. I became my own man, not the one that I was expected to be – but the one I *wanted* to be.

"More complicated than your fiancé leaving you at the altar in front of three hundred people?"

I huff out a humourless laugh. "Probably not."

We each sip our drinks, the silence between us growing. I want to keep her talking, but I'm scared of what else she might say.

"I really wanted to be a mother," she says quietly after a long few beats.

"You will be."

"What if I'm not? What if I've missed my chance?"

"You're only twenty-eight years old; you haven't missed your chance."

"But I have to start over now, what if it takes me years to trust again, then another year or two to meet someone, I might be forty by the time I'm in a position to be ready for a baby, and that might be too late."

She's breathing rapidly, panicking. I refill both our glasses and she downs it all in one go – so I do the same. If she's going to get written off, the least I can do is meet her there.

I know she's grieving the loss of her relationship right now, but it's clearly not just my brother that she considers she's lost, it's the entire future she had planned out... children, a *family*... probably a house with a white picket fence too.

Darcy deserves all that and more. She deserves to

have the future she's always dreamed of. She's hands down the sweetest person I've ever met in my life.

"There's more than one way to skin a cat, Darcy."

"What?" She frowns.

I rake my hand over my face. I'm definitely not the man to have this conversation with her, but I can't seem to stop myself.

"There's more than one way to become a mother. If it is taking too long – which it *won't*, or you never find someone – which you *will*, it doesn't mean you can't still be a mother."

I still don't know how much Darcy had to drink before I got here tonight, but even I'm starting to feel the warmth of this tequila in my veins, so she must be well and truly under the influence. She's about fifty kilos dripping wet, and she's never been much of a drinker, if she keeps downing her drinks like she's doing right now, I'll be holding her hair back while she vomits before this night is through – not that I'd mind – but I'm sure she would.

I pour myself another drink and toss it back, ignoring the empty glass that she's holding out for me.

She scowls at me when I don't fill it for her but doesn't press me on it, so I take another.

"Alright then, *Mr. I know everything*, how am I meant to get a baby without a boyfriend?"

Yup, she's well on her way. Her words are slurred, just ever so slightly and she's started using hand gestures to reinforce her point, plus, the Darcy I know isn't quite so forward. I prefer this less diplomatic version of her. She's been moulded over the years into what my brother wanted her to be, so it's refreshing to know that the real her is still in there.

I lift a shoulder and let it drop. "Sperm donor."

She laughs, but it's not because she thinks it's funny, but because she thinks it's ridiculous. "I don't think so."

"Why not?"

I down another glass of bitter tequila, feeling the effects more by the minute.

"Some random dude I don't know? What if he tried to come back and get to know the kid one day? What if he tried to get custody? What if he had some kind of illness he didn't tell me about?"

"They have rules and tests, Darcy."

She laughs humourlessly again. "You think I could afford to go down the IVF track? You really don't know me too well, do you? I write a column for a magazine, Ryan, I'm not made of money like Jacob. If I was going to get a sperm donor, it'd be some guy whacking off into a cup and then the old turkey baster method."

She's looking up at me with those big blue eyes, deadly serious.

My lip twitches as I bite back a grin. "You're serious?"

"I'm not serious about any of this, but in a hypothetical situation, sure... it's been known to be done."

"That's not right." I grimace.

"Exactly," she says with a roll of her eyes.

She holds her glass out to me again, and this time I half fill it, then watch as she tips her head back, letting the liquid slide down her throat.

"You know... you *could* just do it the old-fashioned way..."

The words are out of my mouth before I can really think about what I'm saying... about what I've just implied.

She raises a brow at me. "You think I should go out and sleep with random guys until I get myself knocked up?"

I shake my head quickly. "No." *God no.* Just the thought of that makes my stomach turn.

She looks at me in confusion, her beautiful eyes glassy.

"No... not some *random* guy." I run my hand through my hair, hating myself already for what I'm about to suggest, but willing to offer it anyway, because this is *her*, it's Darcy, and there isn't a thing in the world that I wouldn't do, no line I wouldn't cross if she asked me to. "*Me*, Darcy... you could do it with me."

THREE

Darcy

I feel my jaw fall open like you see in the movies.

Did he just...?

I *must* have heard wrong. I have to be more wasted than I think I am, because there is no way in hell that Ryan Steele just offered to be my sperm donor.

I climb off the bed in slow motion, and as soon as I'm on my feet, I realise that yes, I *am* that drunk.

Not so drunk that I don't know what I'm doing, but clearly drunk enough that I'm imagining things that can't be happening, because there is just no damn way...

I laugh out loud at myself.

"Darcy?" Ryan questions.

My eyes find his. He's watching me with a mixture of surprise, regret and hope etched into his handsome features – as though he's somehow heard the nonsense going on inside my brain.

"I think I had too much to drink, I could have sworn you just –"

"Offered to be the father of your child?" he cuts me off. "You heard right, Darce."

We stare at one another for what feels like an eternity.

"What the fuck?" The words fall from my lips.

He just shrugs, unspeaking, while his eyes say a thousand different things.

"Are you high?" I demand.

He chuckles, and the sound does something strange to my chest. That's one thing that has never been the same about Jake and Ryan – the way they laugh. I've only heard Ryan laugh a handful of times before now, but each time it's given me this feeling of déjà vu... that sensation you get when something is pulling at a distant memory, but you can't quite connect the dots.

When Jacob laughed, it always felt forced.

"No. I'm not into drugs these days."

I raise a brow at him. "These days?"

"I dabbled in my younger years." He shrugs his shoulders. "But I get the feeling you're veering away from the questions you really want to ask me, Darcy."

I feel myself sway a little bit on my feet, and I shake my head to clear my thoughts.

I need a minute to figure out if I'm having some type of out-of-body experience or if this is all really happening.

I hold up one finger, indicating that I want him to give me a minute.

I sink to the ground and cross my legs under myself – no easy task given the five hundred layers of fabric covering my body.

Jacob left me at the altar... fact or fake?

I glance down at my ring finger and find it bare.

Fact.

I'm in the bridal suite with Ryan... fact or fake?

I look back to the bed and find him sitting on the edge, watching me patiently.

Fact.

He just offered to try and knock me up... fact or fake?

I meet his eyes, and it's all right there.

Fact. Definitely fact.

"*Why?*" I whisper. "Why would you do that for me? Jacob would never speak to you again."

He huffs out a humourless laugh. "I couldn't care less about him; he'd be doing me a favour... but you wouldn't have to tell a soul, Darce."

"I think people might have questions about who the father is, Ryan."

"Then tell them if you want to."

"But imagine what people will say."

"What gives you the impression I care about 'people'?"

I don't know why I'm even having this discussion with him. The answer is *no*. It's the only answer for it. Anything else would be total madness. I cannot let my ex-fiancé's twin brother father my child. I just *can't*. And besides that, *I* could be the reason Jacob and I couldn't conceive – this whole conversation is moot.

Then why do I so badly want to say yes?

"Ryan... I..."

"You deserve something good, Darcy. Something for *you*. Not for anyone but you. If you want to be a mother, if you're ready right now, then you should be a mother. I can't imagine anyone better for the job."

"I don't know..."

"There's no pressure. There's no expiry date. You don't have to decide anything right now."

He really wants this for me. I can see it on his face. He wants me to be happy. Not for appearances. Not for personal gain. It's for *me*.

Fuck it. It's time I thought about me.

It's crazy. It's reckless... and I'm going to do it anyway, I realise.

"Okay," I breathe.

He nods. "You just think about it, and let me know when you've decided."

"No." I shake my head. "Not, *okay I'll think about it*... I'm saying okay, let's do it." My heart is beating so rapidly I'm sure he would be able to hear it from across the room, but it's not in panic, it's in excitement.

I don't know if it's the tequila talking, but I want this. It's time I looked after myself, put myself first – no one else is going to – that's one thing that has been made abundantly clear to me today.

He looks shocked, as though there was no world in which he thought I'd actually agree to this.

I manage a giggle. "It's not too late to back out if you didn't mean it," I say, sincerely.

He shakes his head instantly. "Never."

I feel nervous all of a sudden. I don't know what the hell I'm thinking, maybe I'm not thinking at all. Maybe I should sleep on it, decide when my body isn't pumped full of alcohol and heartbreak, but that approach – living my life with caution is what has led me to this point. Maybe it's time I tried something new.

I've got nothing to lose. Literally *nothing*. It's a sad, but honest realisation.

Ryan is watching me with a focus like nothing I've ever seen before, it's as though my every thought is being displayed above my head in neon lettering and he's simply plucking them out of the sky.

He sees the moment I make my final decision. *Yes.*

"We need an agreement, with rules," I think aloud.

He sips his drink, contemplating my suggestion. "Rules are good."

I nod, even though there is *no* way I'm going through with this. Except that I am. I really, really am.

"We need a piece of paper."

"I've got my phone?" he suggests.

I shake my head quickly and then regret it for how lightheaded it makes me feel. "We have to sign it. It has to be paper."

He smirks, he clearly thinks I'm overreacting, but he gets up anyway and starts opening and shutting drawers, searching for something to write on. "Got a pen." He holds up the pen to show me.

"Paper?" It's a one-word question, but for some reason it sends my heart into a gallop again.

He rifles through a drawer for a moment longer. "I'm coming up empty here, Darce."

I guess couples in the honeymoon suite usually aren't writing notes.

I watch nervously as he goes to the bedside table on the far side of the bed. "This will do."

He holds up a copy of the bible.

"*Ryan,*" I hiss at him. "We're probably already going to hell if we go through with this, we don't need to seal the deal by defacing a holy book."

"You're not religious, are you?"

I shake my head. "No, but –"

"Me neither." He winks at me. "So I figure it's just a book in that case."

My eyes widen as I watch him tear out a page.

"Oh relax. This is a blank page anyway; you can't send me to hell for a blank page."

"Tell that to the devil at the front gate," I grumble to myself.

He slaps the sheet of paper down on the desk and moves around the room to retrieve our empty glasses and the near-empty bottle of tequila.

I watch from my spot on the floor as he pours his to the rim and half fills mine. "Rule number one..." he prompts as he picks up the pen and starts writing.

"No catching feelings," I provide. I've had enough feelings to last me a lifetime, I'm sure as hell not looking to catch any more.

He glances at me over his shoulder, his expression unreadable.

"What?" I shrug at him. "It might not be a problem for you, but I'm a girl. I struggle to separate sex and feelings."

"That's the problem though, isn't it, Darce? You can't catch something you already have."

I frown, not understanding. "*What?*"

"Nothing, just forget it." An emotion crosses his features, a pained look that is gone again so quickly I decide I must have imagined it. I *am* pretty drunk after all.

His focus shifts to the sheet of paper in front of him and he scrawls down the words, the only sound in the room the scratching of the pen as he writes.

"Here I was thinking you were going to insist on

the turkey baster method," he says without glancing up.

I feel my cheeks colour. "Shit... I –"

"Relax." He chuckles. "I was just kidding."

I can feel the deep red staining my cheeks, and I hope like hell that I still have enough makeup on my face to cover it.

His eyes meet mine. "Rule number two?"

I think for a moment. "We do this one time, and one time only."

"What if it doesn't work?"

Then it's probably for the best.

Then you will have got off lucky.

Then you'll never have to see me again.

"Then it wasn't meant to happen," I finally say.

He nods, once, and adds the rule to the list.

"Is that it?" he questions.

I shake my head. "Two rules doesn't seem like enough. One more."

He gestures for me to go on.

"Rule number three..." I get to my feet, my head feeling clearer than before, and stroll around in a slow circle. "This is our little secret," I finally say.

Ryan might not care what people say, but I do. I don't want to be *that* girl. This might work, it might not... Hell, for all I know I might leave town and never come back, but either way, this isn't something we need to share with the world.

I half expect to see hurt or disapproval cross his

face, but he gives me no reaction, instead just jotting down the third and final rule.

"Now I guess we both sign it," he says.

I nod, cross the room and hold my hand out for the pen.

FOUR

Ryan

Her delicate hand signs the sheet of paper, somewhat reluctantly, but without shaking. I'd be impressed if I wasn't so nervous.

She's close enough I can smell her scent again. It's so much more intoxicating than any volume of alcohol could ever be.

She hands me back the pen, those captivating eyes of hers holding me in a trance.

"Your turn," she whispers.

I could be signing my life away here, everything I've worked so hard for is at risk right now, but I don't care. I trust this woman with my life. All of it means nothing in comparison to her. None of it is worth anything without her.

It's the easiest decision I've ever made.

She breaks our connection, and I scrawl my signature below hers without giving it another thought.

"Done."

She steps back as I get to my feet, my height towering over her small frame.

She's anxious. She's shifting her weight from foot to foot, unsure what to do with herself.

I reach for our glasses and offer the least full one to her. "Cheers."

We clink the crystal together and each of us drink until they're dry.

"What now?" Darcy asks quietly. "I don't know how you want to do this..."

I hold my finger up to my lips and step closer to her.

She gasps as I pry the empty glass from her hands and set it down, pulling her flush against me in the next second.

I've imagined this moment so many times. Pictured it so many different ways, yet none of them were ever quite like this.

It's nothing like what I wanted, but somehow, it's still *everything*. *She's* everything. I'm going to savour every second of this.

"I've got you," I breathe.

I cup her face in my hands and tip her head up towards mine.

"You promise?"

"I promise, Darcy. You can trust me. I'll take care of you."

She nods, her eyes fluttering shut as I close the distance between us, doing what I've wanted to do for years and kissing her. *Finally.*

I expected her to be timid... *reserved*, but the second our lips meet, something inside her snaps and she presses herself closer to me, her hands winding up my chest to cling onto my neck.

I press her lips open and sweep my tongue into her mouth, she moans and kisses me back even harder. She sucks my lip ring into her mouth in a way that makes me think it's not the first time she's thought about doing it.

"Jesus, Darcy." I groan as she lets it slip through her plump lips.

"Ryan," she replies, breathless.

I need to be careful here, remind myself where I am and who I'm with. This isn't some meaningless one-night stand. This is Darcy. This is the woman I've been in love with for years.

It doesn't matter that she doesn't feel the same way. It doesn't matter that my feelings are one-sided; I *will* make her feel loved. Because she is. It's that simple and that complicated.

I press my lips gently to her jaw, kissing along her chin and down her throat. She swallows deeply under my touch.

I follow the column of her throat up her neck to

her ear, kissing every inch of skin I come into contact with.

She tastes even better than I could have imagined. She's so fucking sweet.

I know there's a solid chance I'm only getting one shot at this. One night only with her and I'm going to make sure that I savour every second I get, even if it breaks my own heart in the process.

I wrap my arms around her waist and lift her up, still kissing her endlessly as I walk her towards the huge bed.

I can't speak for her, but I feel sober as a judge. The buzz of the alcohol is long gone and the only thing consuming me now is *her*.

"Are you sure you want to do this, Darce?" I whisper against her ear.

She looks up at me, so hurt, so scared, so *beautiful* and nods her head. "I'm sure."

I stare at her, letting my gaze travel from her messy blonde hair to her perfect cleavage.

She watches me, watching her. "*Ryan*," she whispers again; this time it sounds like begging.

I can't stay away any longer. I *have* to have her. I've waited so long to hear my name on her lips.

She's mine now, for this moment. Not his. *Mine*.

I'm a completely and utterly shit human, because when I turn her around and unzip the wedding dress that she chose to wear to marry my brother, I let myself believe that she's wearing it for me.

"You're beautiful." I repeat the two words I said

to her the very first night we met, holding her gaze as I relive the moment I've never quite let go of. They might be generic words, nothing words really, but I wish she could feel them, *remember* them...

I know I'm being stupid, in the world we live in, a woman like Darcy has been called beautiful one million times over at this point.

She's the kind of woman who turns heads when she walks into a room. She has been beautiful for as long as I've known her, and she probably always will be. A simple compliment isn't something she'd recall.

She shudders as I slip the straps off her shoulders and slide them down her arms.

Her back is facing me, and I press a single kiss to the middle of her bare shoulder blades. She's braless, and I'm dying to spin her around and take care of her perfect tits, but I remind myself to take my time.

Foreplay isn't exactly required for this particular arrangement, but hell if I'm not going to make the most of it.

Her dress falls to the floor, and she's standing before me in nothing but a scrap of white lace, her perky ass cheeks peeking out the bottom.

Fuck.

Nothing has ever been so perfect, *nothing.*

I crouch down and run my tongue from the base of her spine all the way up to the top of her neck.

She moans, a breathless, sensual moan, and I'm completely fucked from that sound alone.

I'm fully dressed, hard as a rock, desperate to be inside her.

She spins to face me as my arms surround her, and her fingers claw at the buttons on my shirt, forcing them out of their buttonholes and opening the fabric to her. I shrug out of it, and it falls to the floor at our feet.

I growl as her nails skim across my skin, leaving a trail of fire in their wake.

I lie her down on the soft white bedding, trying and failing to be as gentle as I'd like, not that she seems to mind – her eyes are filled with hunger.

She watches me as I unhook my belt and tug it from the loops on my suit pants, and I stare back at her, taking my fill of her sexy-as-hell body and beautiful eyes.

She shifts, wiggling her hips, and that's when I spot it.

A tiny moon and star tattoo on her hip.

My breath gets caught in my throat.

It can't be.

I swallow, my throat thick.

"You've got a tattoo."

Her eyes dart down to her hip, almost as though she's checking it's still there.

"It's nothing," she whispers as her fingers gloss over the small, inked lines on her otherwise untouched skin.

It's not *nothing* – it's the furthest thing from nothing,

but I can't say a word. I've got a tattoo nearly identical on my body too – not that she'd ever notice it amongst the patchwork of colours and patterns adorning my skin, but it's there... as a reminder of that night.

As if I'd ever need a visual reminder.

FIVE YEARS AGO:

"WHAT ARE YOU LOOKING AT?"

She points up at the clear night's sky, scattered with bright stars.

"Have you ever seen anything more beautiful?"

I nod. I have. I'm looking at something infinitely more beautiful than some yellow dot in a dark sky. I'm looking at her.

"I know it sounds cliché, but looking up at the stars just makes me feel so small. It really puts things into perspective for me, just how tiny my problems really are."

I reluctantly tear my gaze from her and tilt my head upwards towards the sky, trying to see what she sees.

"There's a whole other world out there," I reply.

"One we know virtually nothing about."

"It is humbling," I admit.

"I think so... when my parents were alive, they would always tell one another that they loved each

other to the moon and all of the stars. It embarrassed me as a kid, but now I think it's kind of perfect."

"To the moon and all of the stars," I repeat.

I know right then, in that very moment, after only an hour of knowing this woman, that I'm going to love her exactly like that, forever.

"NO PART of you is *nothing*, Darcy."

I lower my mouth to her hip and kiss the thin lines marking her.

She shudders beneath me, and I smirk to myself. I love the way her body reacts to me – it's completely out of her control.

I kneel between her parted legs and tug down my suit pants, taking my boxer briefs with them.

My dick is raging now, sitting up loud and at attention – all for her. She doesn't miss it either, she's watching with laser focus.

"Lose the underwear," I tell her as I tug off my pants the rest of the way.

Her eyes widen, probably at the commanding tone in my voice, but she lifts her ass and slides them down her legs without comment.

My head drops back as a groan escapes my lips. "You've got the sexiest little pussy I've ever seen. *Jesus Christ.*"

She blushes a deep red on her cheeks and her teeth sink into her bottom lip. She's embarrassed –

shy. She's got no fucking reason to be. She couldn't be more perfect to me if she tried.

I dive between her legs, my arms wrapping around her thighs to hold her in place as my tongue makes contact with her clit.

She arches her back, a cry of pleasure bouncing off the walls around us as I tease and torment her with my mouth.

Her hands find my head and grip onto my hair, pulling and tugging as I bring her to the brink.

Her hips start to wriggle, and I hold her tighter, not allowing her any escape from the orgasm I know is building inside her.

"Ryan!" she cries out. "Fuck, Ryan, I'm –"

I don't stop – I take her all the way there until she's shaking in my arms, her moans becoming louder as she rides the wave.

I gently let go and sit back, grinning at her as she jerks and twitches.

"Oh my god." She pants. "That was amazing."

"Oh, baby, we're only just getting started," I say with a wicked grin.

Before she can even reply, I've lined myself up and pushed deep inside her hot little body.

"Fuuuuck," I breathe as her walls grip me tight and she moans in my ear.

This woman has ruined me already. Nothing has ever felt so good – so right, and as I start to move inside her, filling her deeper with every stroke, I know that nothing else ever will.

———

I WAKE to the sound of a groan and a muttered, "Oh fuck." I'd know that voice anywhere, and unfortunately, I also recognise the torment in the tone.

Memories of last night come back to me in a flood, a rush of images hitting my brain one after the other, each having more impact than the last.

They're so good, but without the influence of alcohol in my system, I can see that this was never going to be as simple as our hastily made agreement led us to believe.

This is complicated. This is messy. This might result in a *baby*.

I feel the bed move and I lift my head, too fast – my vision blurs before I gather my bearings and zone in on her.

"*Darcy*." My voice is raspy as I reach for her arm, stopping her from climbing off the bed. She's got the sheet wrapped around her naked body, the golden skin of her back and shoulders exposed to me. "Come here."

"Ryan, *don't*. This was a mistake."

She just referred to the greatest night of my life as a mistake, and the only person I'm disappointed with is myself for thinking it was going to go any other way than this.

Dreams are free but sleeping with the woman who was meant to be your new sister-in-law was never going to go well for me, especially not when I love her the way I do.

"You can get a morning-after pill, Darcy, you don't have to risk anything you don't want to risk." The words come out numb, dull. *Dead.*

"There shouldn't be anything for me to risk, this should *never* have happened," she whispers.

She's right. I never should have offered. I never should have crossed the line. She was hurt and vulnerable, and I shouldn't have done it.

"I'm sorry," I start to say, but she cuts me off.

"It's not your fault." Her voice is broken and small, but I know she means those words. She doesn't blame me, but she regrets what happened between us and that probably hurts more than if she did decide to hold me responsible for our actions. "My head is killing me. I need to shower. I'm a mess, *everything* is a mess." She's on the verge of tears.

"I can help you. I can take care of anything you need."

She shrugs off my hand that is still lingering on her arm. "I think you've done enough."

I nod in defeated acceptance. She's dismissing me.

"I want to help you." I'm pleading now, and I hate the sound of the desperation on my lips, but I can't make it disappear.

"*Please.*" It's barely a whisper this time. "Just go."

I turn away as she stands, giving her privacy. I

don't turn back until I hear the door to the bathroom shut.

I gather my clothes in silence, putting each item on far slower than required, hopeful that she'll come back out and face me, but suddenly I'm fully dressed, and I can still hear the spray of the shower hitting the floor.

She's not coming out. Not while I'm still here.

I glance around the room, spotting our agreement still on the desk where we left it. I can't help myself. I fold it in half and shove it in the pocket of my suit pants. And then I do something I never thought I'd do... I do exactly as she asked, and I walk away from her.

FIVE

Darcy

The water sprays heavily against the tiled floor of the shower, yet I'm still bone-dry, sitting on the closed lid of the toilet.

I have no idea how much time has passed as I've sat here, thinking through the colossal fuck-up I've just made.

I slept with Ryan.

I slept with my brother-in-law.

Only he's *not* my brother-in-law and he never will be, but that's not the real problem here, the problem is that I liked it.

I slept with another man on what was meant to be my wedding night, and I *liked* it.

Fuck.

I squeeze my eyes shut, trying to shove away the hazy memories from my mind.

The agreement.

The sex.

The passion.

The very real consequences of what might result from last night.

My stomach lurches and I fly off the toilet, only just getting the lid up in time to throw up noisily into the bowl.

I wipe my mouth with the back of my hand as angry tears fill my eyes. I'm so *angry* at myself for being this stupid... this *reckless*.

I close my eyes and let my head fall back against the wall behind me as my forehead pounds from the alcohol I consumed last night.

I don't know what the hell is going to happen from this moment on. *Nothing* is the same as it was yesterday, but I do know one thing. I can't sit on the floor of this hotel bathroom forever.

Eight weeks later

I WISH I could say I hadn't seen this coming, but the two pink lines staring back at me have been waiting to be confirmed for the past month and a half.

I've been sick, moody, my boobs have been *killing* me and I can smell *everything*.

The universe is one cruel bitch when it really comes down to it. Jacob and I tried for just over a year to have a baby... and *nothing*. I slept with Ryan *once* and I couldn't be any more knocked up.

"Two lines means negative, right?" Freya asks with a grimace as she waves the pregnancy test around before glancing at it again to confirm what we both already knew.

I huff out a humourless laugh.

On the one hand, I'm beyond excited that I'm going to be a mother. It's literally all I've wished for since I was a little girl, but I wanted the family experience, not the single mother with a questionable baby daddy package.

This is all kinds of complicated, and a big part of me was holding onto hope that maybe I was having all these symptoms out of stress, rather than it being due to a foetus holed up in my uterus. It's been a brutal eight weeks – not only have I grieved the loss of my relationship, but I've stressed about the choice I made that night.

That's the reason I waited this long to pee on a stick. In fact, I only went through with it today because Freya finally lost her patience with me and demanded that I 'just do it already'.

So here I am, officially pregnant.

"Sorry I'm late, did you check it yet?" Steph calls out as she flies through the door of Freya's apartment in a rush, the door slamming shut behind her.

Freya rolls her eyes at Steph. "I don't know why you even apologise for being late anymore."

"Because it's the polite thing to do." She tosses her bag onto the table as she crosses the room towards us.

"The '*polite thing to do*' would be turning up on time," Freya mutters as Steph plucks the test from her hand.

"I *told* you." She points her finger at me as she takes in the positive result.

I don't answer, just sink further into the couch I've been sleeping on for the past eight weeks and cover my face with a pillow. "What a mess." I groan. "What the hell am I doing with my life?"

"Oh, here we go again." I can hear Steph's disapproving look through her tone. "Pity party for one."

I throw the pillow in the direction of her voice.

"My husband ran out on me at the altar, I have no house, no money and now I'm knocked-up to his fucking brother!" I yell at her.

She throws the pillow back at me. "Get some new stories," she says with a grin. "We've heard those ones already."

I bite back a laugh. Nothing about it is funny really, but that's the beauty of Steph; she can make me feel better about my depressing life in her own way.

I don't know what I would have done without the two women in front of me during all of this.

"So... when are you going to tell him?" Freya asks.

"Well... I was thinking... never?" I reply weakly.

"You can't *not* tell him, D."

"Technically I could."

"Shut up, we all know you're not going to have this man's baby and not tell him, so cut the bullshit and let's make a plan."

"I don't even know how to find him," I argue.

"*Lies*. You Googled him three weeks ago. You know *exactly* where to find him." Freya looks at me with a no-bullshit expression written all over her face.

"How do you know that?" I demand, shocked.

"You borrowed my laptop, sweetie. Google search history is a *thing*."

I narrow my eyes, glaring at her. "Fine." I groan. "I know where to find him. Down at the bar. Jacob never told me that Ryan actually owns R&R's. I thought he just worked there."

"I think there's other things you should be considerably more worried about that Jacob wasn't telling you," Steph quips.

I flip her off with another bit-down grin. Again, it's *not* funny, and I'm still so hurt over what Jacob did to me, but what I never expected was to feel relieved... like I can finally drop the act that I've realised my life had become. I feel more like me than I have in years.

"Okay, so you're going to just head downtown to

his bar and tell him. Easy."

"Oh yeah, that'll be a real barrel of laughs... 'Oh, hi, Ryan, you remember that time we wrote a contract on a page ripped out of a bible? Yeah. I'd like to enforce that. Oh, but I've already broken rule three, and rule two is irrelevant'."

"Hold up, on a page of a *bible*?" Freya demands at the same time that Steph laughs and mutters, "no wonder you're having bad luck."

I silence them both with a death glare.

"*What*?" Freya raises a brow at me. "That's loose, just sayin'."

I sigh heavily. "What's even the point of telling him? He didn't want to be a dad, he just wanted me to be a mum."

"And you're not telling him he has to be a dad. But you can't bring a human into the world that shares his DNA and not tell him about it. It's just not right. He's a good guy, he deserves to know."

She's right. I *know* she is. There's no way I'd do that to Ryan. He is a good man, and I'd never lie to him about something like this or withhold that type of information.

I've been mulling this over for weeks – another reason I've been so reluctant to take a test, because now it's all real and I *have* to do something about it.

Sure, this baby in my belly was just as real yesterday as it is today, but yesterday I still had the luxury of possibly being wrong about it. Today has taken that from me.

"I'll tell him," I confirm. "Would have been great to have a couple of glasses of liquid courage before I did, but that's obviously off the cards now too." I roll my eyes.

"Can we just put aside the slightly odd predicament you've found yourself in for a second and talk about how much that little baby is going to love its favourite aunty," Freya says excitedly.

"His favourite aunt Steph you mean?" Steph says, brow raised.

"*Her* favourite aunt Freya," Freya corrects.

"I'm glad you're both so excited, but can we maybe not count our chickens before they hatch? There's a long time between a positive pregnancy test and a baby, you guys."

"You're right." Steph nods. "*Of course...* you're right. Let's be sensible... But I'm going to buy him his first pair of kicks," she blurts out.

I roll my eyes. Steph and sensible don't really go together in the same sentence.

"Didn't you say you had a meeting this afternoon?" Freya questions.

Steph glances at the watch on her wrist, which may as well not even go, given how utterly useless she is with checking the time.

"Shit. I'm late. Gotta go." She flies out of her chair and kisses me on the cheek. "You're going to be the best mum in the world." She's so sincere it almost brings a tear to my eye.

Steph might be a hot mess, but she's the best

friend a girl could ask for.

"How are you feeling?" Freya asks me as we watch Steph exit in much the same manner she entered.

"Scared, excited... sick." I grimace.

I can't tell if the nausea swirling in my stomach is morning sickness, or dread over the fact that I have to see Ryan again – that I have to tell him I'm carrying his baby.

The scary thing is, I already know what he'll say. I can picture the tender look in his eyes. He'll wear the same expression he did that night.

If I'm being honest with myself, it's not just telling Ryan I'm pregnant that scares me, it's what happens after that. I haven't stopped thinking about the night we shared; I can't forget the way he made me feel.

I can't stop myself from wanting to do it again.

"You really will be great, D, and we've got your back, you know that, right? With anything."

I do know that. The lengths that the three of us would go to for each other is immeasurable. The two of them having my back is the only thing I know for certain these days.

I smile at her, tears of gratitude blurring my vision.

"Do you want me to come with you to talk to him?"

I shake my head. I appreciate the offer, but this is something I know I have to do on my own.

SIX

Ryan

"Rebel?" I call down the hallway into the back room, trying to locate my business partner and best friend.

"Two seconds!" she yells back.

I wait where I am, my eyes scanning the sheet of paper I've just been handed by our bar manager.

We're a relatively new establishment still, but I don't think anyone anticipated what a success we'd be. Thursday through Sunday we're packed to a level that is almost uncomfortable. The booze we brew on site has won us a shit load of awards already and since then, production has gone through the roof to keep up with demand.

It's everything I could have hoped for and more. This place has basically become my entire life, yet there's still something missing that I can't quite put my finger on.

My mind flashes to Darcy's face, and I know I'm lying to myself. I know *exactly* what's missing, but it's something I'm never going to have, so I do my best to ignore it. After all these years, I've got pretty good at that.

It's been eight weeks since the day of her wedding... since the night we slept together.

I spent the two weeks that followed in a zombie-like state, hoping she'd come and find me – tell me she had figured it all out... that she'd realised we were meant to be together.

That never happened.

Once a month passed, I gave up any and all hope. I haven't had a lot of experience with pregnancy in my life, but I know that it doesn't take this long for a woman to get a positive test, or at least a missed period or whatever. That only meant one thing. She wasn't pregnant. It didn't work.

It was all for nothing. I broke my own heart, yet again, and she didn't even get the thing she wanted most in the world out of it.

"I talked to JT about adjusting the temperature for that brew, he's going to do it once he gets done with the dinner rush." Rebel is standing in front of me when I look up.

I hear her, but I've obviously been distracted at some point during the evening, because I have no idea what she's talking about.

"Sounds good," I reply, hoping that's the right answer.

She gives me a brief questioning look before brushing past me and pushing the door open into the bustling restaurant.

We're best known for our in-house brewed beer, but we have a killer menu too.

It's a Wednesday, not one of our busiest nights typically, but most of the tables are filled with dinner patrons regardless.

"Did Andi get the produce order done?" I ask.

Rebel doesn't answer me.

"Reb?"

She's stopped dead in her tracks, staring across the room, her cat-like eyes narrowed.

"I've never actually met the woman, but is that..."

I follow her line of sight as she speaks and everything fades to a blur as I take in the sight of Darcy Shearer, standing inside *my* bar, talking to *my* front of house staff.

Time slows down as Kat points in my direction, showing Darcy where to go, and I meet eyes with the woman who has been on my mind virtually non-stop for far longer than I'd care to admit.

"Ryan?" I feel Rebel's hand land on my shoulder, and I don't miss the way Darcy's gaze leaves mine and sweeps the woman next to me from head to toe.

I might not be an expert when it comes to females, but I can feel the tension between these two, even when they have an entire room separating them.

I've gotten used to the way women look at Rebel – I get it – she's stunning in an almost intimidating way. Bright red hair... tall and curvy, she's hard to miss and even harder to look away from, but her and I have never been anything more than friends. She's like a sister to me. I'd have been lost without her support in my personal life and partnership in the business. That hasn't stopped the very few dates I've had over the years from being incredibly threatened by the main woman in my life.

"Want me to get rid of her?" Rebel offers as Darcy starts to walk cautiously in our direction, a little too much sass in my best friend's tone for my liking.

"Play nice." I murmur the warning. *Nice* isn't exactly Rebel's MO, she's more blunt and brutally honest than she is sweet and charming.

She laughs wickedly. "Maybe I should make myself scarce if 'nice' is the expectation."

"Maybe that might be wise," I drawl.

I feel her walk away, but I don't look after her, I can't take my eyes off Darcy.

If Rebel hadn't have confirmed she was really there, I might not have believed my own eyes. I've wished for this moment for weeks, the one where she walks in the door and smiles at me.

Only, she's not smiling right now. In fact, she looks terrified.

I realise then that I'm frozen in place, standing stock still, waiting for her to come to me like some kind of moron. I force myself to cross the crowded restaurant to meet her, never once looking away in fear she might disappear right before my eyes.

"*Darce,*" I say, my voice gentle as I reach her. "You're here?"

"Hi," she replies quietly, her eyes darting to her feet as she speaks.

"Is everything okay?" I dip my head to try and catch her line of sight, but she's firmly intent on staring at the flooring.

"Could we talk... somewhere private? Or if now isn't a good time I can come back, or –"

Something's wrong. I can tell without her having to say another word. I haven't spoken to my brother since the day he ran out on Darcy and I gifted him with a broken nose for his trouble, but if I had to fathom a guess, I'd say that Jacob has upset her again in some way – she's got the same look in her eye.

"Now is perfect. We could go to my office?" I offer, the words coming out much calmer than I feel on the inside.

Those blue pools finally rise back to mine. "Okay." She nods.

She's as nervous as I've ever seen her, she keeps shifting her weight from one foot to the other and she looks tired, *so tired...* as though she hasn't had a decent night's sleep in weeks.

I rest my hand on her lower back and guide her across the room to the far side, and through the door that leads to the office that Rebel and I share.

It's crazy, the change in the air when we find ourselves alone. I don't know if I'm imaging it or if she feels it too, but the space between us is crackling with energy as we walk silently down the dimly lit, narrow hallway.

She doesn't look back at me as I press my hand slightly firmer against her jacket, showing her the way.

The office is empty when we reach the door and I'm grateful to Rebel that she has made herself scarce. I've got a bad feeling about this whole thing, and I doubt that Rebel's presence would help the situation in any way.

She might be my closest friend, but she has the ability to stir the pot like no one I've ever met, plus she's got the temper of an agitated crocodile, neither of which would prove useful in the current moment.

"Make yourself comfortable."

Darcy walks timidly into the room, glancing around at the framed posters on the walls before taking up a spot on the leather lounge suite on the far side of the room.

I wait, watching her as she fidgets nervously for what seems like forever, before finally stilling and raising her eyes to meet mine.

I quietly shut the door and cross the room towards her, seating myself only a short distance away from her body.

I know that body like the back of my hand. How

warm and inviting it is, how perfect it feels against mine...

I mentally slap myself, now is not the time for those mental pictures.

"There's no easy way to say this, so I'm just going to come straight out with it..."

My breath gets caught in my throat as I wait for her to do exactly that.

Her eyes meet mine. "I'm pregnant."

I feel my head pull back in shock.

Pregnant.

A million scenarios have run through my mind since my gaze landed on her only five minutes ago, yet her being pregnant somehow wasn't one of them.

I'd given up on that possibility – well and truly convinced myself that the idea of me putting a baby in her belly was never going to happen.

"But... but – but," I stutter, "But it's been so long... I thought it wasn't going to happen... I thought –"

"I was too scared to take the test," she whispers, the quiet words having no trouble interrupting my rambling. "I think I knew the whole time, but I was too scared to confirm it."

I feel like I'm in shock. I don't know why my brain is having so much trouble processing this, when it was always a very real possibility – one that I thought *a lot* about. Unprotected sex leads to babies. Everyone knows this.

"I don't know what to say," I admit, letting my

body fall back against the back of the couch, my eyes closing as I try to process this new information.

"You don't have to say anything, you remember what we talked about, right? I don't need anything from you. I wanted a baby, I got one. This is nothing you need to worry about."

I know what's she's doing, she's panicking and she's trying to cut me out. I know what I said that night... that this could work however she wanted it to, but now that it's really happening, there is no way in hell that I'm just going to fade into the background.

It might make me a liar and a lousy human, but this feels like the one shot for me and her. This is my chance to show her how good we could be together. I'm never going to get a better opportunity than the one in front of me.

That, and the thought of this baby, *my* baby, growing up without a father – thinking their dad never wanted to know them, is just not an option for me. I'm in. I'm all in.

"I never said I didn't want to be part of this, Darce."

She sighs. "What I'm telling you is that you don't *have* to be. I can do this on my own. I'll be fine, Ryan."

I know damn well she could do this without me – without *anyone*. I doubt there's a thing in the world this woman couldn't do if she set her mind to it.

"I know you can, but you *won't* be. I'm going to be by your side every step of the way."

Her eyes harden a fraction, and I wonder what it is that I've said wrong.

"Until *when?* Until you meet someone and start a family of your own? A *real* family... I'd rather you were never in the picture to begin with."

The words cut me to the core, not only because I know it's a scenario that will never happen – I'll never have that life with anyone but the woman in front of me, I know that in my heart – but because she really believes what she's saying and it's causing her pain. The last thing I want is to cause her any type of pain.

"I'm not going to leave you, Darcy."

I reach for her hand, to take it in mine, but she pulls away. "That's what Jacob said."

I can tell she intended to use the words like venom, but they come out soft and hurt – just like the woman who spoke them.

I go for her hand again, this time refusing to let her avoid the contact.

"Look at me," I tell her softly. Her eyes slowly lift from her lap to meet mine.

She's so fucking scared. There is blind fear written all over her face. I don't blame her. This is huge – life changing. I'm scared too.

"I'm never going to leave you," I promise in a tone so sincere, there's no way she could possibly doubt me. And she shouldn't doubt me – no promise has ever been so easy to make in my thirty-one years.

"I'll be there, the entire way, okay? You'll get so sick of me you'll be begging me to leave you alone."

A small smile graces her lips. She might have walked in here acting all tough, but on the inside, she's just scared and alone.

Darcy Shearer doesn't fool me. I see through her so effortlessly, it's as though she's made of glass.

She gives me a small nod.

"How are you feeling?" I lightly squeeze her hand. "Have you seen a doctor yet?"

"I've been better. Morning sickness sucks... it could be worse though I suppose."

"You're getting sick?" I demand, outraged for reasons unknown to me.

She giggles softly and my misplaced anger evaporates. "I've been told it usually settles down after the first trimester... but I haven't seen a doctor yet. I only took the home test a few days ago and I've been trying to work up the courage to come and see you since then."

I hate that the idea of talking to me has been such a source of stress for her, but it's done now, and we can move forward. *Together.*

"I'm glad you came."

She squeezes my hand lightly.

"Are you going to tell Jacob?" I ask. As far as I'm concerned, my brother is as dead to me as he's ever been, and hell would freeze over before I felt obligated to share this news with him, but it's not just my call. Darcy gets a say too, and I already know I'd support her either way.

Her eyes widen. "God no."

The corner of my mouth twitches in amusement. I guess we're on the same page regarding my brother.

"I haven't heard from him since he had all of my stuff boxed up and sent over to Freya's a few days after the wedding."

I inhale deeply through my nose, trying not to let my anger about that statement get the better of me.

"You're living with Freya?" I finally ask once I've regained my composure. It's the only piece of information I can take from that sentence that won't cause me to lose my shit.

She tilts her head slightly to the side, her nose wrinkling. "Yeah... I mean, I guess... I've been sleeping on her pull-out couch since I checked out of the hotel we had booked for the wedding."

A *pull-out couch*. No fucking way.

My brother is total scum. He'll be sleeping like a baby in what's likely a plush super-king bed they once shared, while she's over here, slumming it on her friend's couch.

"Have you got somewhere planned to live? An apartment to move into or something?"

I wait, almost hoping the answer to my question is *no*, because then I'll have no choice. I'll *have* to offer her my place. I can't have the mother of my unborn child living the way she is now.

No way in hell.

She shakes her head. "I'm looking, but I haven't really found anything much that I can afford at the moment. I forgot how expensive apartments are in the city... I could look further out, but I don't have a car right now either." Her brow furrows as my anger increases, then she smiles brightly, if not a little forced. "But I'm sure something will come up."

I want to tell her to take Jacob for half of everything – she's entitled to it, she deserves it, but I already know why she hasn't and never would do that. *Pride*. She won't want a thing from him, and I respect her for that. I wish I could still have even a single ounce of respect for my brother, but him leaving her with nowhere to live has just pushed me further toward the edge.

"Come and live with me." The words are out before I can give them even one more second of consideration.

It's not exactly a question, not exactly a demand. It's a statement and I'm unsure how it'll be received.

"*What?*"

She's caught off guard. I've shocked her with my words.

"Come and live at my place. It's huge. There's a big bedroom with its own bathroom – it's all yours if you want it."

"I can't live at your place, Ryan... that doesn't seem right... you and me, sharing a house..."

I huff out a humorous laugh. "I think living arrangements are probably the lowest of the concerns as far as what we're sharing, don't you?" I tip my head towards her stomach, which I note, is still flat.

I don't know if that's how it should be or not. I scowl. My total lack of knowledge about pregnancy is a problem. I make a mental note to consult the internet or buy some books or something.

"I don't know..." she replies quietly, drawing my thoughts back to the matter at hand.

I'm so scattered, my mind is being pulled in a million different directions. Her being here sets off endless possibilities for my future.

Our future.

"It's got a really comfortable bed." I bargain with her.

She looks unconvinced.

"It's the right choice, you know it, Darce. You can't stay on your friend's couch when you're growing a baby. I don't want you to be stressed financially. I've got the space, I've got the means. Let me give you a home."

"What about when the baby comes?" She drags her lip through her teeth.

"Then you *and* our baby will have a home. My door will always be open to you both."

A small crease appears between her eyes, and it takes all of my self-control not to reach out and smooth it with the tip of my finger. "I can't ask you to do that."

"You didn't," I reply simply.

"Can I think about it?"

"Nope," I reply without missing a beat. "Offer expires when you walk out that door."

I'm absolutely full of shit, I'd never turn her away, no matter how long it took her to think it through, but I want her to accept the idea now, not go away and overthink it with her girlfriends for the next week.

Call me selfish, but I'm not willing to wait for the answer. I want her 'yes' now, and there's something about her expression that tells me her resolve is wavering.

"Ryan..."

"Darcy."

"I..."

"Just say yes."

She pauses, and I see my whole life flash before my eyes. It's like everything is somehow riding on this one answer.

"Yes," she breathes.

SEVEN

Darcy

"You know what? I never thought I'd see the day you moved into a house with your sexy, forbidden lover, as knocked up as the day is long." Steph flashes a devilish grin.

I should ignore her. I know she's only trying to bait me, but biting my tongue isn't really one of my strengths, so naturally I snap back.

"First of all, he's not my lover, and secondly, I'm not *moving in* with him... I'm just staying with him until I get my shit together."

She raises a brow at me as she tosses the last of my boxes into the back of her boyfriend Mark's truck. "Whatever you say, sweetie. I've got twenty bucks that says you live happily ever after."

"Stop it." I roll my eyes.

She's been at it all week, ever since I told her and Freya that I'd accepted Ryan's invitation to come and stay with him.

It was more of an instruction than it was an invitation to be fair, but given how incredibly indecisive I've been feeling lately, him giving me no room to overthink it was probably a blessing.

"You should go for it. Ryan is *ridiculously* hot."

I just shake my head at her. I really don't need to be reminded about the sex appeal of Ryan Steele – it's glaringly obvious. I'm pregnant, not blind.

"Is he bad in bed? Is that the problem?"

"*God no.*" The words are out without me even having time to filter them, or the wistful tone in which I deliver them.

Steph smiles triumphantly. "I *knew* he wouldn't be. Spill."

I want to tell her to shut up – that there's no way I'm talking about this with anyone, but part of me has been *dying* to share something from that night. I want to gush over all the details with a girlfriend like I would if it was just *some guy* that I'd had incredibly hot sex with – so I do. I spill it all.

"I keep getting flashes, Steph. The look in his eyes when he was deep inside me... the feel of his hands on my skin. That wasn't a business transaction, and it certainly wasn't drunk, sloppy sex... it was... there *aren't* words."

Steph – the woman who barely stops talking long enough to take a breath seems lost for something to say. I'm a little pleased with myself.

"I've got to ask..." she finally says, "do the piercings... you know... extend below the collar?"

I hold back a groan. That nipple piercing was *so* hot. I never thought piercings were something I'd be into, but I was wrong. So very, very wrong. I don't even have to say anything, my reaction is answer enough.

"But it can *never* happen again," I say as I round the back of the ute and open the door.

"Um, like hell it can't." She follows me and pushes the door shut so I can't climb in.

I scowl at her.

"Don't punish yourself. Have *all* the hot, tattooed, pierced sex." She almost begs.

"I think you're forgetting that Ryan is Jacob's *twin*. You remember Jacob, right? The man I was engaged to marry?"

She waves away the idea with a flick of her hand. "Jacob is a complete dickhead who never deserved you in the first place."

I want to agree with her, because she's not entirely wrong, but my mind flashes to the tattoo on my hip... to the first night Jacob and I met... to random events from over the past five years, and I can't do it – I can't agree with her.

Jacob has two sides, I may not have got to see his

softer side anywhere near as much as I'd have liked to, but it was there. There was a part of him that deserved me. I can't deny that. It wasn't all bad between us.

I shrug a shoulder in response.

She gives me a stern look and re-opens the car door for me.

We drive over to Ryan's without any conversation required on my part. Steph is going on and on about something that happened at work that turned into a scandal between two of her workmates, followed by a very descriptive mental picture of them being caught in the copy room.

I'm only half listening, instead watching her with amusement. She looks ridiculous driving this big vehicle. Mark is huge, and Steph is anything but.

"Next street on the left." I interrupt her rambling as the GPS shows me the way to Ryan's.

I glance around at the houses we're passing and notice for the first time that we're in a really expensive neighbourhood. I'd never given too much thought to where Ryan might live, or how well off he is financially now that he's not part of the filthy rich, family business.

Money never seemed to be his priority over the years I've known him. He wouldn't have walked away from his inheritance the way he did if he was all about money but judging by the size and quality of homes in this area, he isn't doing too badly for himself despite that.

"Lover boy is loaded too, huh?" Steph asks as she dips her head to take in a huge three-storey house as we pass it by.

"It's number thirty-seven," I say, ignoring her comment.

She drives farther down the street and comes to a stop outside a slightly more modest-looking house. It's still *very* nice, and I bet it cost an arm and a leg to buy, but it's by far the least extravagant on the entire street.

I can't quite place my reasoning for the thought, but I'm relieved it's not some giant mansion.

We pull into the drive and no sooner that Steph has killed the engine, Ryan appears out of the front door, a wide smile on his handsome face.

A sigh slips through my lips without permission.

"I agree, mmm, mmm, *mmm*," Steph teases smugly, climbing out of her door before I have a chance to argue with her assumption.

I close my eyes for a minute and take a deep breath. I'm here. I'm really doing this. It's going to be fine.

I *can* do this.

I hear my door open and feel the cool air on my skin. My lids flash open.

"You planning to get out of there anytime soon?" Ryan asks, his tone amused.

I take in every inch of him from his dishevelled hair to his bare feet.

Shit.

Shit, shit, shit.

He looks all kinds of handsome dressed up, but it's possible he might look even better dressed down.

It's as though he Googled 'what to wear to drive women wild' when he woke up this morning and then put on exactly that.

He's got grey sweatpants slung low on his hips and a snug-fitting white t-shirt stretched across his broad chest. His bare arms are littered with tattoos, and I'm suddenly curious to know if any of them have any specific meaning to him, but now is not the time for twenty questions. Now is the time to remember how to function.

I unbuckle my seat belt and climb out of the vehicle on shaky legs, my body brushing past Ryan's as I move.

His lip twitches as though he knows exactly what he's doing to me, and he's enjoying my reaction.

"Thank you again for this," I say as I walk around to the back of the ute where Steph is already unloading my stuff.

"Nothing to thank me for." His voice comes from close behind me. *Too close.*

I resist the shudder that my body tries to let out.

I'm going to have to get my head on straight, and *fast.* I'm going to be living with this man for the next little while, at least, and I can't spend that entire time coaching myself through fighting the level of attraction I'm feeling right now.

I don't know if it's the pregnancy hormones making me crazy or what, but I make a mental note to Google it when I get some privacy. It would be great if I could blame this on something other than pure lust.

Both Steph and Ryan refuse to let me lift a single box or bag into the house, even though I'm perfectly capable, so I stand there awkwardly, watching them carry the few things I own, into my new home.

Ryan shows me to the spare room – *my* room – it's beautiful. The space is so well coordinated I have to assume he had help from a female. The whole house just has a woman's touch, which unsettles me in a way I wouldn't have expected it to.

I can't help but wonder if he shared this home with a girlfriend, a fiancée... maybe even a wife. I know very little of what's happened in his life these past few years.

"The door to the left is your bathroom, and that one there is your wardrobe." He points at the two doors that come off the clean, light room, disrupting my train of thought.

"It's a beautiful room, Ryan. Thank you."

I turn to face him. He's leaning against the door frame, his arm stretched up to rest on the top of the frame. My gaze lingers on his toned and golden bicep.

I don't know how he does it – he makes standing still look sexy.

"You need to work out what you want me to pay in board, I have some cash on me, but I'll set up a –"

His brow sets in a deep scowl and he cuts me off. "Stop talking."

I tilt my head to the side, confused. "What? Why?"

He shakes his head, "I don't want your money. I won't take it."

"You have to, I can't live here for free," I reply, outraged.

"If she's being ungrateful, I'll swap places with her," Steph says, appearing behind Ryan and slipping through the doorway. "This house is *amazing*."

She's obviously been giving herself the grand tour, typical Steph. No boundaries and even less shame.

"I'm not ungrateful, I just can't –"

"Then it's settled," Ryan cuts me off with a firm nod.

Those intense eyes of his are staring at me again, a mix of annoyance and confusion swimming in the depths of them. Mine are probably mirroring back the same.

There is no way I'm going to let this go, if it means I have to track down his bank account number myself, or hide cash in drawers around his house, I'll do it. He's already being so generous with his time and space, the last thing I want to do is take advantage of him financially too.

"Well, this has been fun, but I've got to get going. Mark is waiting for me."

I hug and thank Steph, and with a few inappropriate, sexually based hand gestures behind Ryan's back, she's gone and we're all alone.

"Come on, I'll show you the kitchen and living room."

He reaches his hand out towards me, and it takes me a few seconds to realise that he wants me to take his hand.

He wants to hold *my* hand.

I'm ridiculous. I've had sex with this man, but our palms touching still freaks me out.

I don't know where I find the balls, but I comply, resting my hand in his much bigger one.

He leads me down the hall, my palm sweating in his.

Just a simple touch, something so innocent and sweet has my mind racing and my heart galloping in my chest.

I feel like a teenager on a first date, all hormones and nerves as he leads me through the living room, dining and into the kitchen.

"I didn't know what kind of food you liked to eat, so I got a bit of everything." His tone is sheepish as he drops my hand to open the double doors on the huge pantry in the corner, revealing shelf after shelf of snacks, cereals, treats... it's like a supermarket threw up in here. The gesture is so kind, so generous and also so completely unexpected. "There's fresh fruit and vegetables in the fridge."

"You know, we might have to make another trip, there's not nearly enough options," I tease. "In fact, I think I could eat all this in one afternoon."

He rubs at the back of his neck, his expression still a little embarrassed. "Is it all too much?"

A smile pulls at my lips as I watch him, watching me. I reach out for him and give his forearm a light squeeze "It's the sweetest, most considerate thing anyone has done for me in a long time, Ryan, I appreciate it, really."

Jacob would never have thought to go out and buy anything for me. He probably would have offered to hire someone to do the shopping for us, if I'd asked him to, but he never would have thought about anyone or anything other than himself for long enough to consider doing something so nice for another person.

"I want you to be comfortable here, Darce, it's important to me. What's mine is yours."

It most certainly is *not* mine, but I can tell by the look in his eyes that this is indeed important to him, and given how much he's doing for me, the least I can do is go along with it.

"Thank you. You're too kind to me."

He shakes his head and opens his mouth to argue, but I get in first, snagging a packet of flavoured popcorn off one of the shelves.

"Are you busy? We could watch a movie?"

His answering smile is blinding, so much so that I physically stumble backwards a step, my jaw gaping.

He's so gorgeous, it's almost hard to look directly at him.

"You good?" he asks, his bottom lip working the ring of silver pierced through it.

I nod, my eyes trained on the movement.

Unwise. I tell myself. Staring at Ryan's lips is definitely a mistake, even more so when I can remember the way that cool metal felt against my bare skin. Skin in places that barely sees the light of day.

"Movie," I blurt out like a moron.

"You want to watch a movie?"

I nod, dumbly, unable to string a sentence together if my life depended on it. I don't know how on earth I managed to sleep with this man without completely losing my shit. I can only assume it was the alcohol, and I won't be able to repeat that until this kid evacuates my uterus.

He smirks, the look too good on him. "What do you want to watch, princess?"

I gape as he brushes past me and walks back out into the living room.

Princess.

I'd always wished that Jacob would call me by a pet name, something sweet, or sexy, or even just something silly that showed he'd gone to the effort to think of it. But he never did.

Princess.

It takes at least three full minutes before my legs remember how to move and my brain resembles something other than mush.

I'm in *big* trouble here. Big, tattoo-covered, pierced, *sexy* trouble.

EIGHT

Ryan

I'd always thought that living with a woman would be a massive adjustment – not that any of my past relationships have got anywhere near the 'move in' stage, but still, I never guessed it could be this easy.

Sure, her shoes are always cluttering up the doorway, she's completely changed the smell of the entire house, and she plays godawful girly music way too loud, but my house has never felt more like a home.

Three weeks Darcy has been living with me. Three weeks together in what I hope she now considers *our* home, and I can honestly say without a moment of hesitation that they have been the best three weeks of my life.

I quickly learned that her favourite snack is

popcorn, and that attempting to watch a movie without it was akin to committing some type of sin. I now knew that she hated to cry in front of me, yet she insisted on watching shows that made her teary. I knew that she talked to her best friends on the phone at least once, every single day. I'd discovered that she couldn't cook to save her life and that she was missing her glass of wine at dinner each night. Most importantly, I'd learnt that I loved this woman like nothing else in the world.

She's it for me. She's living in my house, carrying my child. I don't see how life could get any better than this.

"I was thinking about making green curry for dinner," Darcy says as she stares at the crossword she's been working on for the better part of the past three hours.

I've spent the same length of time reading a book about pregnancy and childbirth while being constantly distracted by her little sighs when she can't figure out an answer, and her triumphant grins when she can.

"Why don't you let me take care of dinner?" I offer. "You can finish that."

She pauses, the pen in her hand hovering in mid-air, a slight pout on her lips. "You never let me cook anymore."

"I'd rather you put your feet up."

"You're not a very good liar."

"Aren't I?" I try to hide my smirk, knowing full well that I am a shitty liar.

Her gaze lingers a moment on my lips before flashing to my eyes. "*No*. In fact, you're shitty at it. Do you not like my cooking? You liked those burgers I made last week, right?"

I ponder how to answer for a moment. They were edible, but they weren't a raging success, that's for damn sure. I don't know how you fuck up burgers, but she gave it a nudge.

I've got two choices here – keep bullshitting her and risk getting food poisoning or fess up and tell her that she'll never be cooking in this kitchen again. I decide on the latter.

"Honestly? You've got a lot of strengths, Darcy Shearer, but cooking isn't one of them," I answer, bracing myself for her reaction.

I was expecting a look of horror, or maybe for her to even get upset, what I didn't expect was for her to giggle, and then full-on laugh.

I don't know why, but I'm starting to think the joke is on me somehow.

"I'm *terrible*," she says through bouts of laughter. "Even *I* don't like my cooking."

I don't know what's going on here, but something tells me I've been played.

"Princess, what the fuck?" I demand.

I've been calling her 'princess' more and more, and after she got over the initial shock, I knew she was growing to like it. The light blush that stains her cheeks every time I say it is my favourite part about it.

"Steph made a bet with Freya that you'd be too nice to say anything, but Freya was banking on you eventually cracking and telling me how bad I am."

I glance at the page number of my book, committing it to memory, and then let it drop to the coffee table with a solid thud.

"You risked the lining of my stomach for a *bet*?" I question playfully as I eat up the distance between us.

Her eyes widen as she scrambles off her seat, looking for an escape, her crossword long forgotten.

She darts into the kitchen – a rookie mistake – I've got her cornered now.

She realises her error as I stroll in behind her, completely at ease as her eyes dart around frantically.

"Bet you don't think it's so funny now, do you, princess?"

She giggles nervously.

God, she's so fucking breathtaking. A living work of art, right here in my kitchen.

"Our baby is going to be the most beautiful thing in the world," I blurt out. I don't know where the words come from, but they're one hundred percent true, so I don't really care if they catch her off guard.

A flush of red colours her cheeks.

Fuck, I want to kiss her so badly. I've been holding back this entire time, never making more than a flirty comment or a cocky glance. I've wanted to, God, I've wanted to, but this is Darcy. She's my whole world, and I'd never forgive myself if I fucked it up, but seeing her like this, barefoot, carefree – blushing... I don't think I have any more patience or self-control left in me.

I take another deliberate step towards her.

She doesn't move, doesn't try to bolt. Just watches.

I take another.

"*Ryan*," she whispers as I'm right before her.

"I've been thinking about kissing you for 22 days, princess."

She doesn't speak; her light blue eyes just stare at me, like cut crystal sparkling in the sun.

"I've wanted to kiss you for longer than you'll ever know." I confess another truth she won't comprehend the full reality of.

My rough palm finds her jaw, and she leans her cheek into my touch, her eyelids fluttering closed.

"You're so beautiful, I can't believe it."

"We shouldn't do this," she breathes, but the way she's leaning into me suggests that she's not entirely convinced of that fact herself.

"Give me one good reason why. *One* good reason, and I'll stop."

"It makes things... *complicated*..." she offers weakly.

I huff out a laugh, my thumb trailing gently over her cheek. "How much more complicated can it get?"

I move my thumb lower, to her mouth and over her plump bottom lip. She moans softly.

Fuck.

The sound sends shockwaves to my brain and my cock. Those moans have been on my mind ever since I sank myself deep inside her all those weeks ago.

"Exactly," she replies, her voice slightly stronger. "Am I not enough to handle already?"

Her line of thought pisses me off. I hate the way she views herself as an inconvenience.

"You're not something to be *handled*, Darce, you're something to be *treasured*."

Our eyes meet again, and she softens. She gives in to this energy that we share. She wants me as much as I want her – I can feel it. I see it in the way her breath catches when I come close and her eyes linger on my lips.

I should stop and check that she's really okay with this, but I'm willing to be selfish in this moment. I know what I want, I've always known... and what I want, is *her*. I know I'm good for her. I know this is inevitable.

I dip my head, lowering it to her level and brush my lips softly against hers. She sighs, a relieved sound that has my heart speeding to a gallop.

I press deeper, my mouth melding to hers while she pushes her body forward, leaving no space between us as her small hands grasp handfuls of my shirt.

We kiss for what feels like forever, neither of us

wanting to lose contact. I kiss her until I can barely breathe and my head is spinning, it's so full of her.

She pulls away, her breath heavy as I rest my forehead against hers, her body still firmly in my grasp.

"Go out on a date with me," I half ask, half insist.

"A date?" she repeats.

"A *date*," I confirm, "I want this, princess, *us* – the whole nine yards, for real this time."

"You don't have to do this."

"You think I don't know that? I *want* to do this."

"We were drunk that night, Ryan, it doesn't mean you have to be tied to me for life."

I scoff at how utterly absurd she's being. "I wasn't *that* drunk."

"We drank more than a bottle of tequila between us, there's no way you couldn't have been drunk," she argues with me.

"I brew alcohol for a living, Darce, trust me, it takes a hell of a lot for me to get so drunk that I don't know what I'm doing."

"You *weren't* that drunk?" she asks again, confusion marring her perfect features.

I shake my head.

"Then *why*?" she whispers.

It's only half a question, but I know what's she's asking. Why on earth did I agree to something so reckless... something so crazy.

"Because it was *you* asking. Lines blur when it comes to you, Darcy."

She doesn't have an answer for that, instead choosing to bury her face in my chest.

I kiss the top of her head and wait as patiently as an impatient bastard like me can.

"I don't know what to say," she finally admits.

"Say yes. Just say yes."

She pauses for a few beats before I hear a whispered, "Yes."

"WHAT, so you're *dating* her now?"

I tense my fist at my side before stretching it out to relax.

Chill, I tell myself. Rebel might be my best friend, but I couldn't give a fuck if she understands this or not – she doesn't need to. Nobody needs to understand this but us. As long as it makes sense to Darcy and to me, that's all I'll ever need.

"Yip," I reply curtly.

I might not be able to see the fieriest red head in my life through the phone, but I know she just rolled her eyes so hard at me that they might have actually gone completely back into her head.

"Where are you taking her?"

"Dinner at *Needle and Thread*."

She humphs in reply. Rebel loves that place, so I know I can't lose any points for my choice of location, it's just my choice of date that offends her apparently.

Rebel knows the whole story, every last detail

from the moment Darcy and I met, up until now. I've learnt that it's easier that way – if I ever chose to keep something from Rebel, she'd find a way to extract it from me regardless. Keeping secrets is futile.

Rebel doesn't even know Darcy, but she's never been able to understand how Darcy could have made such a blunder, and she's therefore held a grudge against her ever since.

"She getting fat yet or what?"

I chuckle because sometimes all I can do is laugh when it comes to my best friend and her total lack of tact. "No, she's not really showing yet, but we're just about into the second trimester so she's bound to pop out a bit any time now."

"Listen to that chat, sounding like you know what you're doing."

"Thought I better read a book about it."

"Fair enough. But I still don't see why you need to date her. So you knocked her up, who cares? Doesn't mean you have to marry the woman."

"It's dinner, not a proposal... I'm saving that for the third date."

"Don't even joke," she deadpans.

It irritates me that she's always like this wherever Darcy is involved. I love how loyal and passionate Rebel is, but on this particular subject, I wish she'd just chill the fuck out.

"Well... listening to you bitch and moan about my life choices has been thrilling, but I've gotta split. I've got a date waiting for me."

"Yeah, whatever, just don't come crying to me when it all falls apart."

I refrain from losing my cool. I don't want anything to put me in a bad mood for the evening ahead, so I let it slide. This time.

"Noted. A pleasure as always, Rebel. See ya."

She makes a dismissive noise and then the line goes dead.

I get where she's coming from, I really do. She's picked up the pieces of my broken heart more than once, hell, more than ten times when I've gone through the worst of it, pining for a woman I couldn't have.

But that was then and this is now. I *can* have her now, and it'll take an army to stop me from doing exactly that.

"You ready?" Darcy's voice behind me pulls me from my thoughts.

I spin in my chair, my reply getting lost as I take her in. She's got on a light blue satin dress that make her eyes look fucking incredible and her body look sexy as sin.

"Woah." The word comes out on an exhale.

"What?" she asks quickly, looking down at her outfit as though there's something wrong with it.

"You look... *woah*." I shake my head, at a loss for words.

Her cheeks colour a pretty light pink, and I crave a cigarette instantly. I need to calm my nerves. My heart is racing and my palms are sweating. I'm caught by those crystal blue eyes, locked in. I'm staring down the barrel of the rest of my life and it's the single most terrifying sensation I've ever experienced. I need a hit of nicotine before I lose my shit – but I can't. I gave up my casual smoking the day she moved in here.

Breathe.

This has to be perfect. I can't fuck this up. I couldn't survive losing her a second time.

Breathe.

"I can change if it's too much."

"Don't you fucking dare," I reply quickly. "You're the most beautiful woman I've ever seen." I get to my feet and take her delicate hand in mine. For a gesture so small and innocent, it still shocks me to my core. Her hand in mine sets me on fire, burns me from the outside in, until every inch of me is totally alight.

She bites her lip, clearly embarrassed by my compliment.

"Thank you," she murmurs.

"Did I just hear you take a compliment without argument?" I tease.

I've been giving her a hard time about arguing with me any time I say something nice to her. She doesn't have too many bad habits, but that's one I can't stand. She's *everything* to me, and the fact that she doesn't see it, or has been led to believe she's not worthy, infuriates me.

Another thing I can blame my dipshit brother for, no doubt.

I'll fix it in time. If she hears me tell her every

day, everything I love about her, she'll have no choice but to believe it herself.

She smiles – my favourite sight in the world – before rolling her eyes. "I guess so. This bossy guy keeps telling me off every time I argue. I figured it's just easier to give him what he wants and do what I'm told."

I refrain from groaning. I can think of a million different things that I want, and being 'bossy' and her doing what she's told fits in all too well with most of them.

"Who knew it would be so easy to bend you to my will," I reply, brow raised, insinuation clear as day.

A quiet moan slips through her lips and her cheeks blush deeper red.

I swallow deeply, I can feel my Adams apple bob in my throat.

I run the back of my finger slowly down the side of her face. "I think... that we better leave this house right now, before I get so carried away that I can't."

It's her turn to swallow deeply now as she gently nods. "I think that might be wise."

NINE

Darcy

"Cheers." He holds up his mocktail glass to clink it against mine. "To us."

I can't help but laugh – he's so rugged and manly, the fact that he's holding a fruity, pink and orange drink that contains not a drop of alcohol but does have a pretty little pink umbrella in it, is hilarious to me. But he insisted.

I'm not drinking alcohol, so neither is he. Apparently, it's as simple as that. I've just learnt that he doesn't mind the occasional cigarette from time to time as well, but that he threw out the pack the day that I agreed to come and live with him.

I don't know what I did to deserve someone so

incredibly supportive in my life, but whatever it was, I couldn't be more grateful.

Ryan is more than I ever could have imagined or wished for. It feels wrong to think it, because I doubt he'd like the comparison, but he's all of Jacob's good parts, mixed in with even more amazing qualities of his own. I'm struggling to find a flaw with the man.

"Anything else you've been secretly giving up out of sympathy?" I tease as he sips his drink and then looks at it in surprise.

He shakes his head. "Nope. Just the drink, smokes and my bike."

He says it so causally it takes me a minute to register what he's said.

He picks up his menu and starts glancing over it. "What do you feel like eating? No shellfish for us, you better add that to the list of things I'm giving up."

"I'm sorry, can we just back up for a second here?"

He looks up and frowns at me. "You can't have shellfish, princess, it said in the book. And no soft cheeses." He frowns as he looks at the menu again, no doubt scanning it for soft cheeses now.

I giggle at the concerned look on his face. He's so sweet, I almost can't handle it. I found him reading a pregnancy book the other day – he looked so sheepish, as though I would have expected him to be an expert with no need for a book. Truth be told, he's probably more informed than I am – I'm still living in a state of denial about how this baby is going to get out of me and into the world.

"Not about the seafood." I shake my head in amusement. "About the bike."

"What about it?"

"You don't ride your bike anymore?" I push.

"Nah, I'm selling it, so I don't want to tick up any more miles." His focus shifts back to the menu. "The chicken sounds like a bit of me."

"Ryan!" I half yell, half laugh. "Put the freaking menu down for five seconds. I know you're hungry, but I need to know why the hell you're selling your bike. I thought you loved that thing."

He looks at me as though he doesn't understand my confusion but sets the menu down on the table. "Because I'm going to be a dad," he replies, as though it should be obvious to me.

"What does being a dad have to do with you not riding a bike?"

"*Everything*, Darce." He meets my gaze, and I melt at the tenderness there. "I haven't ridden that bike since the day you told me you were pregnant. Those things are a death trap, I've got responsibilities now – a family to take care of. I don't want to take that kind of risk for a thrill."

I don't know if I'm overwhelmed by his total dedication to me and our baby, or if it's pure pregnancy hormones, but I feel my eyes turn glassy.

"Don't you dare cry," he warns me, a smile playing at the corners of his mouth.

I think it's too late to be stopped, but I try and blink back the tears that are threatening to spill over in the middle of this crowded restaurant.

"I know it's over the top and stupid, and I know plenty of parents still ride, but I'm happy to give it up. It's nothing to me. Plus, I know you hate them."

He's right, I'm not a fan of bikes, they seem so fast and dangerous, but I don't recall ever telling him that. It confuses me sometimes; he knows things about me that I have no recollection of ever talking to him about. We've barely even had any real conversations, just small talk at events before he left Steele Industries, and very few other occasions after that.

"Will you take me for one last ride?"

I don't want him to sell the bike – it's part of who he is, and who he is, is pretty great. So if I can get him out on it again, with me, maybe I can convince him that it still has its place is his life – used sensibly of course.

"*You* want to go for a ride?" he asks, already smirking.

"Hey! I ride," I reply, trying my best to sound sassy and convincing.

He laughs. "I bet you've never ridden on a bike in your life."

"Well, you'd be wrong." I resist the urge to poke my tongue out at him. "I went on a bike when I was ten years old one time at a carnival."

That only makes him laugh harder. "That doesn't count, Darce."

"Well then maybe you better take me out so I can tick it off my bucket list." I smack at his hand playfully. He's full-on laughing at me now.

"Well, you've given me no choice." He makes a show of wiping amused tears from his eyes. "Where do you want to go?"

"The beach," I reply without even having to think twice. "Take me to the beach please."

"The beach it is, princess."

I honestly think I could have said I wanted to go to the moon, and he would have promised to make it happen just as easily.

He picks up his menu again, and this time I don't disrupt him from finally being able to choose what he wants to eat. I just watch. I memorise all the little faces he makes, the rise of his left eyebrow as he reads. The way his Adam's apple bobs as he sips his drink. The way he cracks his neck every so often, how he turns the silver ring through his lip... all the little things that make him, him.

I'm starting to fall for this man, I realise.

I can't even believe it's happening, after everything I've been through, I honestly never thought I'd feel anything close to love again, and certainly not this soon, but I have feelings for Ryan. Real, genuine feelings, and more than that, I can't picture my future without him anymore.

I can see our baby crawling through hallways and pulling things off shelves, and when I imagine that, I imagine it in his house. His hallways. His shelves. The three of us together.

"What are you going to get?" he asks me, breaking me from the best daydream I've ever had.

I shrug my shoulders and feel my cheeks blush. I've had the menu in front of me for several minutes now, but the only thing I can think about tasting, is him.

———

I GLANCE at my reflection in the full-length mirror. These tight, black jeans aren't going to fit me for much longer, so I'll be damned if I don't get an appropriate amount of wear out of them before that happens. They're the only pair I've got that can make my ass look half decent and, for all I know, they'll never fit again.

I grab my leather jacket off the bed and leave the room.

I might never have been for a real ride on the back of a motorbike, but I'm pretty sure I look the part at least.

Maybe if I try to look and act like a badass, Ryan might be less likely to treat me like I'm made of glass. Maybe he'll handle me the way he did that first night we were together.

A flood of warmth blooms in my belly just thinking about it. But that's all I've done – think about it.

All thinking and absolutely no action.

Our dinner on Tuesday was perfect. Hands down the best date I've ever been on in my life. Ryan was sweet, charming, funny, and he looked like a god. The only thing missing was a real kiss. He hasn't kissed me again since that day in the kitchen. Sure, he walked me to my bedroom door and gave me a sweet peck on the lips, but I want more. I'm craving *more*.

My body, my mind, my heart... it all wants more.

"Fucking hell." I hear his choked voice behind me, and I spin around to find him stalled in the doorway.

Still channelling my inner badass, I do nothing but raise a brow at him in question.

"Those things should come with a warning label." He's staring at my ass.

His eyes sweep me up and down again.

"You like?" I ask as I slip on my jacket and strut towards him.

I watch as he swallows deeply, his head bobbing up and down with a nod. This must be what it feels like to be him on a daily basis – to wield your sexuality like a superpower. He makes me turn into a ball of mush and hormones more often than I'd care to admit, but it seems like now it's my turn to hold the reigns.

"You look incredible." He growls as I pass by him, my shoulder brushing his arm intentionally.

I give my hips a little more sway than usual on my way to the front door. "You coming?"

I hear him groan.

I like this. This is fun. I haven't felt the power of having a man eating out of the palm of my hand in a long time. Since before Jacob. I changed when I was with him, and it's only been recently that I've realised just how much. I used to be playful, fun, confident... whereas with Jacob, I became... *compliant*.

The scary part is that I'm not even sure how I allowed that to happen. I guess I was infatuated with him – more specifically, the idea of him. I wanted to please him.

I pause outside, the sight of the huge, shiny bike parked in the drive making me rethink this whole idea. It's *massive*. I can't imagine even being able to get on that thing without assistance.

"Where's all that sassy confidence gone now, princess?"

His warm breath at my ear startles me. I hadn't heard him come up behind me.

"That's a big bike."

He chuckles.

"I'll look after you, just slide your arms around me like this..." He slips his arms around my middle, and my stomach flutters with butterflies. "And hold on tight." His mouth is at my ear again, sending shivers racing up and down my spine.

I wonder if it'll ever stop being like this, or if his touch will always be able to excite me this way – set my body on fire and make my head spin.

"The beach is waiting, Darce."

It's only then that I realise he's circled around to the front of me and I'm standing here, eyes shut like an idiot.

My lids fly open, my cheeks heating.

He chuckles again, a smirk settling on his lips. So much for the idea of him eating out of the palm of *my* hand. Hell, at this point, I'd eat off the floor for this man. It's a real new low for me.

He doesn't say another word, just takes my hand and leads me to his bike. I stand still as he fits a helmet on my head and adjusts the strap.

He puts on his own and swings his leg over the leather seat, before settling there like it was made just for him.

Holy hell.

There is no way he's selling this thing. If nothing else, he can just get it out of the garage and sit on it every now and then while I watch.

"On you get, princess."

With a little wariness and a lot of help, I manage to get my leg over the bike and my body wedged in behind his.

"Hold on." I can hear him chuckle as I immediately wrap my arms around him and cling on like I'm holding on for dear life. Which I basically am at this point.

He flips down the visor on his helmet, and the bike roars to life beneath us. If I thought it was intimidating before it's *nothing* compared to now. This thing is scary as hell. It's vibrating like crazy, and the engine is so loud I can barely hear myself think – which is probably for the best. If I could think straight right now I would probably come to my senses and get off. This probably isn't a sensible activity for a pregnant woman.

I open my mouth to say something – who knows what, but my words get taken away with the wind as he pulls out of the driveway and onto the street.

I know we're only going slow, but I cling onto him even tighter and bury my face into the back of his jacket, it's warm and soft and smells like him. It makes me feel safe – even on this death trap.

I feel the hum of his laughter against my cheek. The bastard is *laughing* at me. I don't really blame him; I started so confident and full of myself and now I probably look like a baby koala clinging onto its mother's back.

I don't look up, but I feel when we hit the open road. The bike speeds up and the blur passing by out the corner of my eye goes by even faster than before. I know he's not going that fast – he's being cautious because I'm on the back, but I've still never felt so free. It's exhilarating. I feel like we're flying.

All too soon, we slow down, and I feel the difference in the ground beneath us. We're on a gravelly track now, and I can smell sea salt in the air.

I pry my face off his back, my arms still tightly wrapped around his middle, and tip my head back to see the sun through the visor on my helmet.

He pulls to a stop, kills the engine, and pulls off

his helmet, shaking out his hair and running his hands through his short beard.

God, he's so sexy I can barely stand it. I'm aching for him to touch me, to kiss me... to feel his skin against mine again. Twenty minutes with my thighs wrapped around him has done nothing to dull the desire coursing through me.

He runs his hands over mine, and I feel goose-bumps pebble over my skin, under my jacket.

I reluctantly loosen my hold on him, and he climbs off the bike, looking every inch the god he is, as he does it.

I don't understand how I've never looked at him like this before now... how I didn't see that the uncut version was so much better than the preppy one.

He reaches forward, unclips my helmet and gently slides it off my head.

I don't say a word, I can't stop staring at him. I probably look like a hot mess, but I don't care.

"Are you alright?" He holds a hand out for me, the other supporting my elbow as I climb off the massive machine.

I nod.

"You sure?" He looks at me in concern, probably waiting for me to puke.

I'm so much more than alright, I'm alive, I'm on *fire* – burning for him.

I nod again. "But if you don't kiss me soon, I think I might spontaneously combust."

"*What?*" I've clearly shocked him with my train of thought.

"I didn't stutter, kiss me already. I'm *dying* over here."

He chuckles and rakes a hand through his wavy hair – an action so sexy it should be illegal. "I was trying to take it slow."

"Didn't feel like taking it slow in the kitchen the other day."

He groans at the memory. "*Exactly*, Darce, I rushed it. I don't want to miss all the steps in between, just because we've taken a giant leap right to the end result. I feel like now I need to go back and fill in the gaps. Dating, holding hands, kissing. I just don't want you to miss out on any of it, princess."

Be still my beating heart.

"I'm not missing a single thing. I've got everything I want right here." I tug him towards me and wrap my arms around his middle. He pulls me closer, his strong arms enveloping me.

"You're sure?" he asks as he runs the tip of his nose up the length of mine.

"I don't care about social conventions, or the way things are meant to go – we've got our own thing. I like what we have happening here."

"Yeah?" he questions, teasing me by leaning in closer so our lips are nearly touching.

"Yeah," I whisper. "I'd like it a lot more if you'd ki–"

I don't even get to finish my sentence before his

lips are on mine. His tongue slips into my mouth at the same time that he lifts me, my legs wrapping around his. He steps forward and rests my ass on the seat of the bike.

It's quite possibly the hottest thing I've ever done – making out on a motorbike on a public beach – it only seems fitting that I'm doing it with the hottest man I've ever met.

TEN

Ryan

"Do they mean anything? Or did you just pick out things you liked?" Her finger traces lightly around the lion on my forearm, her touch so feather-light, she's barely making contact, yet somehow it still gives me shivers.

I know she's curious about my tattoos, my piercings... my drastic change in career and lifestyle, but she's never pushed me too far for answers, which is just as well, given that explaining that, would mean revealing secrets I've kept buried for five years.

"Some of them have a story, some of them are just things I saw and impulsively had done. The lion means courage, dignity and strength to me. The sword on my leg was from when I got too pissed with the boys one night and one of them bet me I wouldn't do it."

She giggles and shakes her head at me. "I like them. They suit you. Even if I think you're crazy for betting with tattoos."

I think she's right. This appearance does suit me. I may have gotten my first tattoo and piercing as an act of defiance against my father and brother and their perfectly groomed, immaculately presented, bullshit public front, but every bit of ink I've had etched into my body since has been for me, because *I've* wanted to carry it on my skin forever – or on the rare occasion, because I'd been drunk enough to think it was a good idea.

This is who I am – who I was meant to be. Everything might have gone to shit for me over the years at times, but I can't deny that I never would have found my way here, to the real me, if it hadn't.

Everything happens for a reason – I learnt that the hard way, but I learnt... and look where I am now.

"I noticed you had a tattoo yourself..." I gently probe.

I remember that I mentioned it on *that night*, but I've never asked her about it until now. I'm dying to know if it means what I think it does.

I'm probably overthinking it. Her and her girl-friends probably had too many cocktails and all thought it would be cute to get matching moons and stars. It's probably nothing to do with what she told me the night we first met at all. But it might be... and I *have* to know.

"I just have the one."

She's leaning against me now, and I can't see her eyes, but I can hear the slight change in her tone.

"Any meaning behind it?"

She nods. "Yeah, just something sweet my parents used to say to one another. You probably think it's silly... but they would tell each other they loved the other *to the moon and all of the stars*. They kind of gave me an unrealistic standard on love to live up to."

"I like that story," I tell her, even though it feels like a rock has formed in the pit of my stomach. I'm full of energy I don't know how to channel. Elation... disappointment... fear... *hope*.

"Me too." I can hear the smile in her voice. "I told it to Jacob once... it felt like an important moment for me. For *us*," she shrugs, "but I guess I was romanticising things again, because he never even put two and two together with my tattoo."

My heart is galloping in my chest. She got that tattoo not only for her parents, but for me. The reason Jacob doesn't remember is because she told *me* that story, not him.

All these years, all this time... I've thought about that moment between us, and now I know for certain that she has too.

It's fucked up – she doesn't know the half of it, but I still feel ecstatic, almost giddy. It gives me hope that maybe one day she'll know everything – and she'll understand.

"Are you okay?" she asks suddenly, and I can't blame her for being alarmed. My heart is going ape shit. It's beating so fast it's probably slamming into the side of her head.

"I'm good. Fine, *really*." I cringe at my choice of phrase. I couldn't be less 'fine' if I tried. "Tell me about your parents," I say quickly to distract her from my obvious lie.

I know her parents aren't alive, but I've never heard the full story of how or when they passed away.

She starts tracing patterns and lines on my arm again, I assume in an attempt to distract herself from the pain this story is bound to cause her.

"They were killed in a car accident when I was fifteen," she says, her voice heavy. "A truck lost control, skidded through an intersection and ploughed right through their car. They never stood a chance."

My skin chills.

I can't even imagine how she must have felt when she heard that news. She was only a teenager.

I kiss her forehead. "I'm so sorry, Darce."

"Me too." She whispers her reply, "I was meant to be with them. We'd been to visit my gran, and I remember I begged and begged to stay behind with her. I don't recall why I wanted to stay there so badly, but they eventually gave in and told me they'd go back into town, do their errands and come back for me in a few hours... only, they never came back."

I feel goosebumps forming on my arms as I think about her or her gran receiving that phone call. It must have been the worst day of her life. The knowledge that she survived that time in her life goes a long way in explaining to me how she's built so tough now. If she handled that, she can probably handle anything.

"Where did you live after that?" I question. I feel like I need to keep her talking. Even though what she's telling me is horrible, I'm hanging on every word. It's all more pieces to the puzzle of the woman I love, and I want to have every single last piece. I want to know it all.

"With my gran. She's my mum's, mum. I lived with her until I was about nineteen, then it was time for her to go into a rest home. I went to college and studied journalism. I visited her all the time. She passed away when I was twenty-six. Dad's mother died before I was born, and his father lives so far away that I've never really known the man." She shrugs. "I've got no siblings, so it's just me now."

Her friends... *me*. We really are all she's got.

"You have a family now, Darce. It'll never be *just you* again."

Her hand instinctively goes to her stomach and rests on the tiny little bump that's barely visible.

I lay my hand on top of hers – a show that not

only will she have the company of our baby, but she'll have me too. *Forever*.

I knew from that first night that I wanted forever. I never would have predicted it to go like this, but this is the hand I've been dealt, and I'll take it. Hell, I'd take it one hundred times over if it meant the end result was her here with me.

I lean in as her eyes meet mine, and I know she registers my intention before our lips meet. A small, soft, satisfied sound escapes right before I kiss her.

She's normally shy and timid, so when she grabs hold of my neck and twists her body to climb into my lap, it's the absolute last thing I expect.

My body catches up long before my mind does, my hands weaving into her hair and tugging on the lengths as her plump lips meld to mine.

A deep growl works its way up my throat when she sinks her teeth into my bottom lip, tugging it roughly into her mouth.

I don't know who the hell this fiery little woman is, but I like her a whole hell of a lot. Her hands are flat against my chest, her nails sinking into my t-shirt and through to my skin, just enough to drive me wild.

"Jesus, Darcy." I moan as she shifts her mouth to my neck, kissing and nibbling.

She lifts her hips a fraction and then lowers herself again, her centre directly over my rock-hard dick.

I completely lose my cool when she grinds her hips against me.

She's on her back before she can even register the action. I hover above her, unsure about the baby she's growing inside her, but she takes care of that for me by dragging my full weight onto her body.

"I want you, Ryan."

Words, for a time, I never thought I'd hear.

"You want me? Or you want this?" I ask as I thrust our lower halves together.

"You. This. *Us*. I want it all," she says, a slight hint of desperation in her tone.

I already know I'll give her whatever she wants. I'd give this woman anything. Literally *anything* within my power to give, is already hers. This is certainly within my power, but I'm not going to push it – not tonight. She might have lost all will power, but I still have some left.

"I'm already yours."

She pauses, her grip softening. "I'm scared."

"Scared of what?" I whisper, my voice dropping to match hers.

"Of *feeling*."

I chuckle softly, my thumb tracing her jaw. "I think it's a little bit late to be worrying about that."

"It was the first rule, Ryan."

My mind flashes to the torn page in my top drawer – our agreement.

If only she knew. I broke that rule the moment my pen touched the paper.

"Look at me, princess, do I strike you as someone

who gives a fuck about rules? I'm wherever you are. It's that simple."

She doesn't say another word, but she obviously believes me. She kisses me again, different than before – she lets go – finally.

"Sleep in my bed tonight," I say between kisses.

She nods, pulling me in to kiss her again.

And when I finally pull back to suck in a deep breath, I see the rest of my life staring back at me.

———

I ROLL OVER, feeling around in my big bed for her, but coming up empty.

"Darce?" I mumble groggily, still reaching around blindly.

I find nothing but empty space. I roll over. I can smell the scent of her on my pillows, so I know I didn't dream up last night – she's been here, cradled in my arms.

"Princess?" I call out again.

My eyes adjust to the darkness, and I see the dim glow of light from down the hall.

I roll back over and climb out of bed, following the light. It's coming from Darcy's room – more specifically, under her bathroom door.

I'm just about to knock on the closed door and ask why she didn't just use my bathroom when I hear her retch and then noisily throw up.

Fuck. I don't bother knocking.

She's wiping her mouth with the back of her hand when I lay eyes on her, wearing my t-shirt, curled up on the floor.

"Ryan," she says in surprise, her voice embarrassed. "You don't need to see this."

I ignore her, coming farther into the room, worry filling me so deeply I can barely think straight.

"Are you okay?" I ask, crouching down next to her, my hand going straight to her forehead.

"I'm fine, it's just morning sickness," she replies. "Really, just go back to bed. I'm good."

Like hell. I'm not going anywhere.

"It's not morning," I say dumbly.

She gives me a small smile. "Technically it is, but I don't think the baby knows how to tell the time yet anyway."

She reaches for a towel, and I grab it for her, helping her wipe her face.

I feel so powerless as she retches again.

She must see the fear and helplessness in my eyes. "It's okay. Happens most nights. I'll be fine, I promise."

"This happens all the time?" I reply in outrage. "Why didn't you tell me?"

I had no idea and I feel like shit about it. I've always been a deep sleeper, so it doesn't surprise me that I wouldn't hear her moving around in her bedroom, but the fact that she's never said a word about her being up *most nights*, sick, isn't okay. This is something I *need* to know.

She smiles at me, and this time it touches her eyes. She's amused by my outrage – even though she's sick. "*Why?* So you could see me all sick and disgusting and fuss over me like you are right now?"

"Yes," I reply, exasperated.

"*No.*" She giggles.

"Well guess what, princess, I'm here now and I'll be here holding back your hair or whatever the fuck you need, every damn night until this baby learns better behaviour."

"Honestly, Ry, it's fine. I'd rather you didn't see me like this."

"Not happening."

She rolls her eyes. She's going pale again, if I was a betting man, I'd be willing to put my money on the fact that she's about to chunder.

I scoop her up under her arms and take her weight for her as she empties what must be the last of the contents of her stomach into the bowl.

There's nothing glowing or magical about this part of pregnancy, that's for damn sure, but I don't care – I want to be by her side through all of it, the good and the bad.

"I think I'm done," she says, her voice tired.

I help her stand and then wet a face cloth with warm water to wipe down her face.

She reaches for her toothbrush and cleans her teeth, all the while watching me through the mirror.

"What?" I finally ask.

She spits out the last of the foamy toothpaste and smiles at me. "You really are something else."

"A shit boyfriend is what I am, sleeping like a baby in the next room while my woman gets sick every night."

"Your woman?"

"Fuck yes, *my woman*."

"Boyfriend, huh?" she muses, looking more and more amused by my caveman act.

"Doesn't seem like enough, but I'm trying not to scare you off." I chuckle as I pull her close and bury my face into the crook of her neck.

"I stink," she mumbles, her neck arching of its own accord to allow my lips easier access.

"You don't."

"I've just been spewing my guts out. I stink."

I chuckle, pulling away.

"I'm going to take a quick shower."

I open the glass door and flick the water on for her. "Can I get you anything?"

She looks at me sheepishly but shakes her head.

I can read her like a fucking book. She wants something, but she doesn't want to ask.

"Tell me," I demand, twisting my lip ring with my tongue.

"I'm good."

"Tell me now or I'm going to stand her and drive you crazy until you do."

She debates it for a second. "I feel like fried chicken."

"Home-made or that greasy takeout kind of stuff?" I reply, not missing a beat.

I couldn't give a fuck what she wants – no matter how inconvenient or unreasonable. If my woman wants fried chicken at two in the morning, then she'll get fried chicken at two in the morning.

"Home-made," she replies shyly.

I lean in and kiss her lips, ignoring the fact that she thinks she smells bad, and then turn, leaving her to shower in peace.

"Where are you going?"

"To make the chicken," I call over my shoulder with a grin.

"*Unbelievable*," I hear her mutter.

ELEVEN

Darcy

"I can't believe I can't come to the scan," Steph grumbles. "I thought we were best friends."

I twirl a strand of hair around my finger as I console her over the phone. "I know, but we'll get pictures and I'll call you right after and tell you *everything*."

"I want to know *more* than everything."

I roll my eyes. "More than everything. Sure, that seems like a reasonable request."

"You know what I mean!" She's pouting, I can tell. "Are you sure you don't want to take me instead of your boyfriend? I can be there in five minutes."

A laugh escapes my lips. I doubt that Steph has the ability to be anywhere within five minutes. I'm not even sure she'd be able to make it from her bedroom across to the bathroom within that time frame.

"Quit being a brat," I scold her. "And I'm not sure if he's my boyfriend. I don't know what he is."

"Well, he should be. Has he kissed you again yet? Have you had any more dates?"

"Yes. And we're going out tonight," I mumble, grateful for the change of subject, but wary of it all the same.

"Where is he taking you?"

"I'm not sure. It's a surprise."

"Handsome *and* romantic. Dayyyuummm girl! Wife him already."

I roll my eyes. "You're not using that expression in the right context. Or at least not with the right title."

Ryan chooses that moment to walk back into the waiting room of the clinic, and I can't help but wonder if he's somehow overheard Steph on the phone. His expression looks amused, and quite frankly, a little smug.

"You should get some action before you're out of action, if you know what I mean."

I feel myself blush scarlet. I could seriously kill this woman sometimes.

"Gotta go, I'll call you after," I reply quickly, hanging up before she even has the chance to reply.

I toss my phone into my handbag as though it's a live grenade, because if I'm being honest, with

Steph on the other end of the line, it may as well be.

"You alright, princess?" Ryan asks, a sexy smirk pulling at the corner of his lips.

"Steph," I say by way of explanation.

He nods knowingly.

We might not have been in each other's lives for that long, but my two best friends have made themselves right at home, and Ryan has got to know both of them quite well. Freya comes over at least three times a week, and I'm starting to question if she's even coming to see me anymore or if she just wants to take in the sight that is my gorgeous baby daddy.

"Are you sure you want to find out the gender?" he asks me for what I'm guessing is about the one millionth time.

I want to know – if it's not too early to tell, and he was willing – as per usual – to give me whatever I wanted. I'm starting to wonder if he'd prefer not to know, but he refuses to say anything that confirms my suspicion.

"You mean, have things changed since you asked me fifteen minutes ago?" I question innocently.

He chuckles. "Fair call, I'll shut up."

He takes my hand gently in his, like it's something that comes so naturally to him, he doesn't even have to think twice about doing it.

He's so sweet and sensitive, a harsh contrast to his rugged, sexy exterior. One look at him and you'd be willing to sell your soul to the devil, just for one taste, but Ryan Steele would never let me sell my soul. He'd never even let me get my hands dirty.

I feel safe with this man, I realise suddenly. It's a strange feeling. *Safe.* I can't remember the last time I truly felt that way.

"Darcy Shearer?" a nurse calls my name from the doorway, a warm smile on her face as I raise my hand.

Ryan snags my bag off the floor and insists on carrying it for me. He's so ridiculous – sweet, but ridiculous. I'm hardly a whale at this point, I barely even have a bump protruding from my abdomen – I can certainly manage to carry my own handbag.

We follow her into the room where Ryan is quick to introduce himself as the baby's father – he's so proud it almost brings a tear to my eye.

She instructs me about where to lie down and what to do, and then she leaves us to it with an assurance that the doctor won't be far away.

"I'm nervous," Ryan blurts out as I get settled onto the bed.

"Why?"

"I'm going to see my baby. My son or daughter. That's massive."

His eyes are wide, I can practically see the nervous energy thrumming through his body.

"You know there's no pressure, if you're having second thoughts..."

He's next to me in less than a second, one of his hands woven into the hair at the back of my head, forcing my face to meet his as his other hand rests tenderly on my stomach.

It's such a stark contrast – the two actions – one rough and commanding, the other sweet and gentle.

He presses his lips to mine, and I have to stop myself from pulling his lip ring into my mouth.

He pulls away long before I'm ready for him to stop, but stays close, refusing to release me from his hold.

"I've never wanted anything as much as I want you and this baby, Darce," he confesses, his voice gravelly and raw.

I can feel my heart thudding violently against my rib cage. I can't possibly deny the sincerity in his tone, but this feels like a dream. I never thought I could feel this way about Ryan – Jacob's brother, but here I am, falling – *fast*.

"We don't always get what we want," I whisper, trying and failing to hide the intense vulnerability coursing through me.

He shakes his head.

"Fuck that. I'm tired of not getting what I want. It ends now."

My breath gets caught in my throat. He's so all-consuming I can barely breathe.

A knock at the door startles me, and I try to pull away as Dr. Davis enters the room, but Ryan barely budges an inch, just loosens his grip on my hair, so he's cupping my neck instead.

"Hello, Darcy, it's nice to see you again."

"You too. This is Ryan – the baby's father. Ryan, this is Dr. Davis."

Ryan scowls a little at my choice of words. After his intense declaration only a few minutes ago, it's clear to me that he wants to be more than just the baby's father, but that's something that's going to have to be dealt with at another time.

Dr. Davis stretches her hand out in his direction, and he finally releases me, giving me room to breathe, yet somehow leaving me craving his touch the second his skin leaves mine.

They shake hands. "Call me Courtney, please."

"Glad to finally meet you, Courtney."

I'd had to meet her on my own a few weeks back – Ryan was out of town on business, and he's been moping around like he missed out on something vitally important ever since.

He's sweet like that; he doesn't want to miss a thing. Not one moment has passed since I told him I was pregnant, that I've felt like I was doing this alone. He's on my side – my *team*. We're in this together in a way I've never experienced before. I can ask for anything, and I know, no matter how extravagant the request – he'll make it happen. He'd move heaven and earth for this baby, and he or she hasn't even entered the world yet.

Dr. Davis – because I can't bring myself to be on a first-name basis with a woman who is getting so up close and personal with my downstairs region – starts preparing the necessary equipment.

She lifts my shirt and squirts freezing-cold gel onto the skin on my abdomen, before spreading it over the small bump with the wand of the ultrasound machine.

I feel Ryan take my hand again, but I can't take my eyes off the screen that has just flickered to life in front of me. The picture is grey and grainy, but I see it clear as day – my tiny little baby.

"And there's the heartbeat," Dr. Davis says as a thudding, whooshing noise fills the room, solid and steady.

That's my baby's heartbeat. *Our* baby.

"That's our baby," Ryan chokes out, his thoughts mirroring mine.

I reluctantly drag my focus from the screen to his face. His eyes are welling with unshed tears. I know this is a moment that neither of us will forget for the rest of our lives.

He leans in and places a soft, sweet kiss to my forehead, and I melt. I can feel another piece of my resolve slip away. I'm *falling* and I'm not sure there is anything I can do to stop it.

"Everything is looking great here. Baby is measuring right on track for the dates. The heartbeat is strong. Congratulations, your pregnancy is progressing well." Dr. Davis pulls my thoughts away from my romanticising, her bright smile reassuring me.

I hadn't allowed myself to think of anything but positive news as far as the baby went, so it's not until

I hear the confirmation that everything is okay, that I realise how worried I'd been that something might not have been normal or healthy.

Ryan squeezes my hand as we both watch our little peanut wiggling around on the screen.

"I'll print you out some images to take home."

"We were wondering if we could find out the gender today?" Ryan asks.

"I'll take a look." Dr. Davis twists the wand around on my stomach again, a slight pinch to her brow as she turns her head to glance at the monitor. "Too early to tell I'm afraid, you should be able to find out when you come back at twenty weeks."

"Ah, what a shame." He grins at me, his expression a little smug, confirming my suspicions that he would prefer not to know.

I fight the urge to poke my tongue out at him. "I can wait another seven weeks."

TWELVE

Ryan

She's dreaming – about our trip to the beach if I had to guess. She's murmuring about sand and her toes, and she keeps making soft moans, the same as she makes when I kiss her – something I've done a lot of the past few days.

"Water... too cold," she mumbles.

I grin. She is definitely dreaming about the beach trip.

I glance at my watch; I can let her nap for about another five minutes and then I'm going to have to wake her for our date.

It's a surprise, and a risky one at that.

I'm taking her somewhere that I've wanted to take her since the day we met, but I never got the chance. I'm terrified that she'll figure it out, but I'm also just as worried that she never will. She's told me the story – *again* – about her parents at least, but still. This has been something I've wanted to do for a lot longer than a month.

I don't know what happens when she knows the full story – which I've vowed to myself she will, one day. She might resent me. She might think I'm crazy for keeping my mouth shut for so long.

She stirs again, her lips pouting softly, drawing my attention to them.

Those lips, they'll be the absolute death of me. They're so soft, warm and inviting... so sweet and irresistible.

I want her, *God* do I want her. I've never wanted anything so badly, but she's not just some woman... she's *the* woman – the one I want for the rest of my life, and that thought – the idea of having her forever is the only thing keeping my complete lack of patience in check. There's no rush – we've got forever to go. Sex can wait.

With another glance at my watch, I decide waking her can't wait any longer – we've got to go, or we'll be late for our booking.

I sweep my hand over her face. "Wake up, Darce, we've got to go, princess."

She groans as she comes to from her sleep.

I feel bad for planning something so late at night, given how tired she is all the time, but it would have been a bit tricky to do this in the daytime.

I get her shoes for her, help her put them on, then hold her hand out to the car and while we drive. It's not until we pull into the car park that I think she might finally be actually awake. She's adorable, sitting there all bleary-eyed and groggy from sleep.

"We're here," I tell her.

I park the car and round the front to meet her at her door.

She glances around, her brow slightly furrowed until she spots the sign against the side of the building.

"The observatory?" she asks excitedly, letting me lead her towards the front doors of the building.

"You want to see the stars? It's a perfectly clear night."

I can tell by the look on her face, she's blown away. "The moon and all of the stars," she whispers.

I nod my head, I know exactly what she's referring to, but I don't say anything.

She pauses and I can tell she's battling with something inside her brain.

"I'll be right beside you, princess," I reassure her.

She looks up at me, right into my eyes and nods her head. "Thank you... I just... *thank you.*"

I know this can't be easy for her. I knew it would make her think of her parents and remember their love, but that's a good thing – things like this keep memories alive.

I usher her inside and we're taken into the room with the huge telescope.

"It's one hundred and fifteen years old," I whisper in her ear as she looks around the domed-ceiling room in awe.

"Really?" she asks, eyes wide.

I nod. "And pointed at the moon – have a look."

She steps slowly up onto the step stool and leans in, gingerly placing her eye on the telescope.

"Oh my gosh," she breathes. "That's *incredible*. It's so clear and it looks so close."

"It's amazing, right?"

"Have a look," she insists.

"You finish up first."

Little does she know, but this is far from my first visit to this observatory. For about six months, I came nearly every week.

I know that view of the moon better than my own reflection sometimes.

"This is amazing, Ryan, thank you."

My chest fills with pride at the authenticity in her praise. I knew she'd love it here.

"Can you see the craters?"

"I can see *everything*. I can't believe that's the moon."

I know what she means, I couldn't believe it either, the first time I saw it. It's as though it's right there in front of you.

"My parents would have loved this."

I reach for her hand and grip it tightly as she stands still, her eye still glued to the telescope.

I stand there with her for what feels like long hours and short seconds at the same time.

"You look now," she finally says as she steps down, allowing me a turn to see.

She doesn't let go of my hand, and even though I've seen this all before, it feels like the first time with her small, warm hand in mine.

"It makes me feel so small," I say, really throwing caution to the wind. They're the same words she said to me that first night, when we stood in the garden bar and looked up at the stars.

She doesn't reply, but her grip tightens and then loosens again.

"Let's go and see the stars," I suggest.

I take her to the other large telescope and show her 'The Big Dipper', 'The Little Dipper', 'Orion', 'Taurus' and 'Gemini'.

She looks at each so excitedly, I feel like a little kid.

I adjust the telescope again. "And there's Mars."

She looks again, gasping quietly as she sees the planet.

"Ryan?" a voice behind me says. I turn around and see Stu, an older guy who spends a lot of time here. "Long time no see," he says when he confirms it's me.

Guess my cover is about to be blown.

I introduce Stu to Darcy and make small talk for a couple of minutes while she goes back to studying the stars.

Stu could talk the back legs off a donkey on any given day, but he seems to get the memo tonight that I need time alone with my girl, so he disappears again after not too long.

I turn back to Darcy, knowing I'm about to get grilled.

She steps back, eyebrow raised in accusation. "Why do I get the feeling this isn't your first time here?"

I chuckle nervously and rub at the back of my neck. "I might have been somewhat of a regular at one point," I admit sheepishly.

She shakes her head at me, a hint of a smile toying with her lips. "Just when I think I have you figured out, you throw me a curve ball."

I cross the small space between us and pull her into my arms. I'm nervous that she'll ask me *why* I'm a regular here, why I came in the first place... that she'll ask me anything at all that might reveal too much.

But she doesn't, she just looks up at me with an emotion in her eyes that I can only place as love... admiration... adoration. This woman is looking at me like *I* hung the moon and all of the stars above us, and I know without having a mirror, that I'm looking at her the very same way.

This is it. This is the moment that I saw coming five years earlier. This is the feeling that I never thought I'd get reciprocated.

I think she feels it too – that this moment is

pivotal – she shifts her weight nervously from foot to foot.

I smile. I like the fact that she's as nervous as I am.

"I'm falling in love with you, Darce." It's not entirely true, I'm already head over heels, but it's a step in the right direction.

She swallows deeply, never breaking eye contact, "I'm, falling in love with you too."

My chest feels so full, it could explode.

I lean in, brushing my lips softly against hers. I couldn't think of anywhere in the world I'd rather be than right here with her, under the moon and all of the stars.

———

WE FALL THROUGH THE DOOR, giggling like a couple of lovesick teenagers who have been dying to get their hands on one another since the moment they locked eyes.

She bites her bottom lip, looking up at me in a way I can't even describe. Her eyes, those light, crystal blue eyes are filled with so much longing. No one has ever looked at me the way Darcy does.

I press her back against the front door at the same moment as she wraps her arms around my neck, tugging my mouth to hers with so much urgency I nearly fall to my knees.

I moan into her mouth as her teeth find my lip and tug gently.

She's so fucking sexy, I can barely believe that she's here, with me, letting me kiss her and touch her in all the ways I've always dreamed of.

"You're so fucking beautiful, Darcy Shearer," I tell her, holding her gaze. "In here." I kiss her temple. "And in here." I dip my head to kiss below her collarbone, over her heart. "And out here too." Lastly, I kiss the tip of her nose. "You're the most beautiful person, on the inside *and* the outside."

It's cheesy as shit, but I don't care. I'd get it sky written right over the middle of this town if that's what it took to make her smile. I'd play out every cliché movie scene, listen to an entire Taylor Swift album... *fucking whatever.*

She presses her body against me, making no secret of where her head is at. She wants me, almost as much as I want her.

I might not have been *drunk* last time, but I wasn't exactly sober either, so I'm going to make the most of being with her this time, I'm going to make sure I remember every single second of this.

"I want you in my bed," I tell her, my tone firm, leaving no room for negotiation.

She doesn't even try, just turns and heads in that direction. I slap her ass as she goes.

That fucking ass. She's been tormenting me with these fucking jeans ever since we went for a ride on my bike. They fit her like a glove and make her ass look sexy as sin.

She giggles, her pace quickening as I follow her down the hall and into my bedroom. No sooner has she stepped over the threshold, I'm in her space again, crowding her.

She's so tiny compared to me, and I love the way that makes me feel... like I can protect her.

"*Ryan*," she breathes as I run my fingers down her sides. She shivers as I make contact with the bare skin between the bottom of her top and the band of her jeans.

I love hearing my name come from her lips. It makes me feel like a rock star, it's pure euphoria.

This is by no means a first in my list of sexual encounters, but it's a first of kinds with her. Everything hits differently when it's with her. We connect on a level I never knew existed until our paths crossed.

I've never been a big believer in soul mates or the idea of everyone having a perfect match, but standing here, with her in my arms; it's hard to deny the concept. She's right for me in every way imaginable.

"Lift up," I instruct.

She complies, lifting her arms above her head.

I reach for the hem of her top and pull it slowly over her head, revealing a black lace bra underneath.

I take it all in, every last inch of her bare, golden skin as I let her top fall to the floor.

I run my finger slowly from her chin, down

between her tits, over her teeny, tiny bump, all the way to the button on her skin-tight jeans.

I slip the button through the buttonhole. "Do you know what they say about a woman's underwear, princess?"

I look up from her jeans to her face. She shakes her head.

I smirk at her. "That if they match, it wasn't you who decided to have sex."

Her cheeks flush slightly, a soft pink colour. "I can tell you right now, they *definitely* match."

I groan as I slide down her zipper and see for myself the truth in her words. I shimmy her jeans down her hips, revealing a pair of barely there, lace underwear.

With a little help from her, I get her jeans off and discard them on the floor in the same fashion as her shirt.

I'm standing in front of her, fully fucking clothed, and I've still never felt desire like this. I'm almost shaking with the need I feel for her. It's consuming me, but I'm fighting it back – I need to explore every inch of her... savour every moment.

"You've got a hell of a lot of clothes on, biker boy," she says, her voice raspy as I continue tracing patterns on her skin, lingering slightly on her small star and moon tattoo.

"I can think of a way to remedy that situation," I growl, shrugging off my jacket and reaching behind my neck to tug my black t-shirt off over my head.

Her hands immediately go to my skin, her fingers splaying wide over my tattooed torso, skimming and exploring in much the same way as mine did hers.

"You are so *hot*." She groans.

I don't know what it is about the way she says it, but I chuckle. She's too fucking sweet.

She leans forward and sinks her teeth into my peck, not hard enough to draw blood, but definitely hard enough to leave a mark. *Sweet* goes out the window and is quickly replaced by red-hot sex appeal as she soothes the bite with her tongue.

Sexy as hell.

Her hands find the buckle of my belt and before I can even take another breath, it's undone and she's sliding down my fly.

"Lose the pants."

It's my turn to do as I'm told now, and it's a request I'm only too happy to comply with.

I drop my jeans to the ground and kick them clear.

"And here we are again," I murmur. Standing before one another with next to nothing covering our bodies.

"Here we are," she repeats.

I back her up towards the bed until she stops, her thighs hitting the mattress. She sits and then lies back.

"I've barely even touched you and I'm going *crazy*, Darce. *You* make me crazy."

"You make me crazy too."

I spread her legs and kneel between them. "I've been dying to taste you again." I cup her between her thighs, feeling how wet she is for me already.

"I'm all yours." She pants.

"Fuck yes you are."

I hook my fingers into the sides of her underwear and drag them down her legs.

Perfection.

"I need you," she begs, "you can taste me later."

I can't argue with that.

I lower myself down against her body before pushing back up to my knees and ridding myself of my boxer briefs. "Condom?"

"I'm already pregnant," she replies, her voice impatient.

I'm well aware she is, but I don't want to be the guy who just assumes.

"Get back down here, right now," she demands as she pulls my arm, unbalancing me. I fall on top of her, catching my weight on my elbows.

I don't need to be told twice, I kiss her, hard and fast, my tongue skimming her lips.

She wastes no time, reaching between us to grip my hard length and guiding me inside her.

Fuuuuck.

This feels like heaven.

She moans in my ear, and it spurs me into action. I start moving, burying myself to the hilt with each thrust.

"*Ryan*," she breathes as I hitch her leg over my shoulder and pound into her.

She grips onto my shoulders, her nails digging into my skin.

I love that shit. "Scratch me," I demand.

She complies, her nails skating down my back, no doubt leaving a trail behind.

I keep up a relentless pace, her moans becoming louder and louder with every passing second.

I throw her other leg over my other shoulder, and she cries out. I'm so close to blowing my load, but I refuse to come until she does.

"Come for me, princess."

She throws her head back.

I wrap a hand around her throat and a guttural, appreciative sound escapes her.

"I'm. Going. To. Come," she manages to get out between thrusts.

I wait until I know she's fallen off the edge before following right behind her, filling her up.

"Fuuuuuck!" I grunt with my release.

I fall onto her.

"Oh my god," she whispers.

Oh my god indeed.

THIRTEEN

Jacob

"Jacob, get in here." My father's booming voice crackles through the intercom system sitting on my desk.

I grind my teeth in irritation but rise from my chair. I've been summoned. I'm well known as being a grade-A prick, and it's no secret where I learnt my ways.

The apple didn't fall far from the tree. Not in my case anyway. My good-for-nothing twin brother is another story, but he's as good as dead to me these days.

I push open my office door, ignoring the questions my assistant is firing at me as I stride across the room towards my father's office.

It's three times the size of the one I currently occupy, and it's going to be mine the second I can get the old bastard to retire like he should have done three years ago.

"Sit," he barks as I enter, not bothering with pleasantries or to even look up from the screen in front of him.

I take my time, an attempt at defiance – but eventually give in to the fact that I'm going to sit – as instructed.

He taps away on his keyboard, as though I'm not sitting in front of him, waiting.

Conrad Steele is a real bastard. Powerful and intimidating. Ruthless and cunning. Men want to be him, and women want to be under him. I've heard the murmuring in the hallways. "Silver fox" is the most common one from the hordes of middle-aged women that work in the building.

I don't give a fuck how handsome the old man apparently is, when I look at him, all I see is the person standing in the way of me running the cutter – like I was born to do. He's nothing more than an inconvenience to me now.

"You fucked up," he grunts, as he finally drags his eyes from his computer and gives me his focus.

"Can you be more specific?" I drawl. I'm in no mood for guessing games. I'm always fucking up in the eyes of my father, so it could take some time to figure out exactly what he's referring to, and time is not something I have in abundance. Time is money in this industry, and money is about the only language I'm interested in speaking.

"With *Darcy*. You fucked up. It's not dying down; the press is still having a field day with the story of the billion-dollar, second-in-charge walking out on his fiancée on the day of their wedding."

I'm well aware of this fact. It's been over two months, and this is a scandal that just refuses to die down.

I'm still being hounded by reporters and magazine journalists almost daily.

It is bad press, I'd be the first to admit that, but I was choosing to run with the age-old mantra that any press was good press.

"It'll blow over eventually," I reassure him.

"Not good enough," he snaps. "I want it remedied. *Right now*. That woman did wonders for your image. She's *wholesome*. If you look good, this company looks good. CEOs don't make waves like this, Jacob. You know there's no way I can hand over the company to you when your personal affairs are in such a state."

The last comment has me sitting up straighter in my chair. I can see where this is going. He's blackmailing me. I sort this mess out, or he'll refuse to hand over the reins.

I open my mouth to argue, but snap it shut again. I learnt at an early age that there was little point in arguing with my father. Once he's made his mind up about something, that's the end of it.

"What do you want from me?" I grind the words out.

"Get her back. Keep her happy. Go through with the goddamn wedding this time."

This is un-fucking-believable. Yet, I should have seen it coming. Everything is about the business. The image. The money.

I should have known better. I should have just married her in the first place, but arrogantly, I assumed I made my own rules. Clearly, I was mistaken.

"What if I can't?" I demand.

"Find a way. No one says no to a Steele."

I can't find an answer inside my brain that isn't a string of profanities, so I say nothing, I simply stand and exit the room.

"Make it happen, Jacob – or kiss your future in this company goodbye," he calls after me.

FOURTEEN

Ryan

"I've got the night off, do you want to spend it together? We could go shopping for baby stuff before the store closes?"

Her eyes light up, but she shakes her head no. "Steph is coming over to watch a movie, I thought you'd have work... but we could all watch it together?"

I don't miss the fact that she's avoided the question about baby shopping. I'm not stupid, I know exactly what's going on. She's worried about how much it will all cost.

There's no way I'm going to let her, or our baby, miss out on anything they want or need, but Darcy is stubborn – and proud. It's not that I don't understand it; she's come from a relationship with Jacob, where she was a kept woman. She doesn't work as much as she used to, no doubt my brother's influence – there's nothing that intimidates that man more than an independent woman. Finances are bound to be playing on her mind.

"What girly crap are you two watching?" I tease.

"Probably something awful if Steph has any say in it."

"Maybe I'll go work in my office." I make a show of standing up, but she grabs my hand and pulls me back down to the couch before snuggling in closer.

"You're not spending a night off away from me. And I know you secretly love a chick flick anyway."

"Wildly untrue." I scoff.

"I heard you singing along to *Pitch Perfect* the other night, you don't fool me."

I nip her in the ribs with my fingers. "Don't repeat that, you'll absolutely kill my street cred."

She giggles and arches out of my reach. "I forgot that you're so big and bad and have a reputation to protect." She rolls her eyes dramatically.

"You bet your sweet little ass I do."

I lay hands on her again, tickling her sides where I know it makes her squirm the most.

She shrieks, trying and failing to stop me.

"Ryan!" she cries.

"Promise you won't tell," I insist.

"I promise, I promise!"

I stop, chuckling as she catches her breath and shoots me daggers with her eyes.

"You know I hate being tickled." She playfully smacks my arm.

"That's what makes it so much fun." I smirk.

She settles back in the couch, one hand on her cute little baby bump, the other on the remote, and she scrolls through Netflix, no doubt looking for the most girly movie on there to torture me with now that I've crossed the line with tickling.

I don't give a shit what we watch; I'd sit through anything for this woman.

I slide a hand in next to hers; it's still hard for me to believe that she's growing our baby in there. It's incredible when you think about it. A human growing inside another human. *Wild*.

"If you put on *Fifty Shades*, I really am leaving," I warn as she pauses on the title.

She giggles, her eyebrow raised in challenge, but thankfully she keeps scrolling.

"What about –" Her sentence is cut off. "Did you feel that?" she demands.

Her eyes are wide in shock.

She gasps, and this time I feel it too. The baby – it's kicking.

"Holy shit."

She nudges my arm, her eyes still wide. "No swearing in front of the baby, if we can feel it, surely it can hear us."

I chuckle and immediately feel another flutter under my palm.

"I think the baby likes your laugh," she says in wonder.

"We need a nickname for this kid," I tell her. "I'm sick of saying 'it' and 'the baby'."

"I've been using 'peanut'," she murmurs, still sitting motionless, waiting to feel another flutter.

"Peanut it is." I nod.

I hear the front door open and shut.

"Come on, Peanut, kick for Daddy," I coo at Darcy's stomach.

"The baby's kicking now?" Steph asks excitedly as she breezes into the room and takes in the two of us snuggled on the couch.

Darcy nods her head in short, sharp bobs. "For the first time just now."

She lets out an excited shrieking noise, kicks off her shoes and makes a beeline for us.

"Get out of the way, baby hog, it's my turn."

I chuckle, and reluctantly move my hand out of the way for Steph to have space to lay her hand on Darcy's stomach.

"Hello to you too," Darcy teases.

I smile as I watch Steph slide in next to her. I love how comfortable she and Freya are here. Neither woman feels the need to knock or ask to get a drink or something to eat. They make themselves at home – because they can feel that this is Darcy's home, and they're a package deal, the three of them.

I wouldn't have it any other way.

I just hope that one day Rebel might be a part of this too. She's my best friend, and even though I'll be completely and utterly outnumbered, I wouldn't really mind. Life would be pretty much perfect.

"Why isn't it doing anything?" Steph pouts after a minute of nothing.

"She was contemplating watching a kinky movie the first time it happened; maybe we should put on some porn?" I suggest with a smirk. "Might get things moving."

"We are *not* watching porn," Darcy deadpans, giving me a 'watch yourself' look.

I know the baby has kicked again because both women's eyes fly to Darcy's stomach.

"I felt it!" Steph says. "Your baby is a little horn dog."

"Steph!" Darcy scolds her. "Don't call my baby a horn dog."

"Fine," she replies, sassily. "But it doesn't make it any less true. One mention of porn and it's having a party in there. I bet it's a boy. No girl gets *that* excited about porn."

I can't help but laugh at the horrified expression on Darcy's face and the utterly convinced one on Steph's.

I don't say it out loud, but I'd love a boy – if nothing else, it would help balance out numbers around here.

"You really are something else. I can't wait for

you and Mark to have a baby one day. I'm going to make *the most* inappropriate comments."

She leans back in her seat, tucking her feet under her bum. "Don't you be putting that out into the universe. You might be happy growing a bun in your oven, but I'm not ready. I can barely keep myself on schedule let alone a small human as well."

I chuckle and take the remote from where Darcy has left it lying on the couch. I'm pretty confident Steph can't keep to any type of schedule whatsoever, but I'm not about to burst her bubble.

"*Men in Black?*" I suggest hopefully.

"No," they both reply in unison before going back to their conversation which I tune out. There's only so much girl talk my masculinity can handle.

"*Shooter?*" I try.

I don't even get a reply, just matching 'absolutely not' looks.

"*The Notebook?*" I joke.

"Excellent choice, Mr. Steele," Steph replies, snagging the remote from my hands before I even register the action.

"I was kidding." I reach after her, but she's already pressing play.

Darcy just giggles and gives me a look. "It *was* your idea." She shrugs.

"Honestly? You're going to make me watch *The Notebook?* Shall I just give you my balls so you can keep them in your purse?"

"I could put them in mine, they can keep Mark's company." Steph smirks.

Darcy shakes her head in amusement and wiggles her butt forward to get up. "I'm making popcorn."

I rest my hand on her thigh. My princess… no movie is complete without a bowl of warm, buttery popcorn.

"I'll get it. You stay and catch every second of this girly crap. I'd hate for you to miss even a glance at Ryan Gosling."

She grins at me, more than happy with that deal.

"So much for not being a fan, you know the actor's name." Steph smirks.

I flip her off, get to my feet and head for the kitchen. Hell, maybe I'll whip up a three-course meal while I'm in here – anything to try and salvage the last part of my manhood and get me out of tearing up about a love story.

———

"YOU'RE UP EARLY." I kiss the top of Darcy's head on my way to the coffee machine.

She's sitting on a stool, a cup of tea next to her and her laptop open.

I don't know what time she woke, but when I opened my eyes this morning, she was gone from next to me.

"Thought I'd make a start on this week's column."

I pour a cup of black coffee and turn back to face her.

"What's this one about?"

"Fast fashion. It's encouraging people to think before they buy. To buy more sustainable products and items that are more diverse."

"I'll look forward to reading it."

She nods her head at me, and I can tell by her expression that she doesn't believe I'd ever read her articles.

Little does she know, I have every magazine that her writing is featured in, from every week since the day I met her. They're collecting dust in a big box in my garage, but I have them and I've read them all. Every single one.

Ever since she told me what she did, with such passion, I've hung on her every written word.

FIVE YEARS AGO:

"WHAT DO you do for a living, Clark?"

I smirk at the use of the character name. I tried to tell her my real name earlier, but she told me to shush, that'd I'd 'ruin it' or something.

"Family business," I answer vaguely.

She raises a brow at me but doesn't push it further.

"What about you, Barbie?"

She smiles. "I write for a magazine. I only get a

weekly column right now, but I work behind the scenes on a lot of content for the magazine and also with some of the authors who are publishing through our sister company."

"You're a writer." I nod. That fits with what I know of her so far. I bet she's brilliant.

She scrunches up her nose. "Sort of. I only have one little column. I'd love to get into some of the bigger articles, and I've always dreamed of writing a novel one day. Maybe a thriller... or a mystery. I have a lot of ideas, I just don't know if anyone would want to hear them.

"I want to hear them," I reply simply. "I want to hear them all."

"I'VE BEEN THINKING about asking for some of my hours back... I gave up pretty much everything else I was doing, except my column... I was just thinking maybe I could do a little more. Working from home of course." She lifts one of her dainty shoulders in a half-shrug.

She's watching me carefully, gauging my reaction. It takes me a minute to understand why she's acting like she needs my approval.

Because she needed his.

I bet she gave it up for my dipshit brother and his out-of-control ego.

I can just picture him strutting around, telling her that she didn't *need* to work. He wouldn't have liked her independence. I'm sure he would have much preferred that his pretty little wife be at home, waiting for him every night with dinner on the table.

He wouldn't have wanted her to work – and she would have complied.

Instinctively, I want to tell her that I'm more than happy to support her financially now and for the rest of her life if that's what she wants, but I don't think that *is* what she wants. She's telling me exactly what she wants – I just have to listen.

She wants to be treated as an equal, and in her mind, that means contributing to the finances, however unnecessary that might be in my mind. This isn't about me, this is about her.

"Sounds good, princess. Can't hurt to ask, right? See what they have available that interests you," I reply casually.

She brightens instantly and releases a nervous breath.

I swear to God, every single day this woman shows me another little part of her that Jacob has broken or cracked. It makes me want to peel the skin from his bones and pull him apart piece by piece. He *abused* her. He might never have laid a finger on her physically, but he's emotionally damaged her, and it's up to me to find a way to help her put those pieces back together.

"I mean, they might not have anything, or whatever, but it's worth asking. They might need help with the manuscripts," she rambles excitedly.

"You could always start working on a book of your own."

Her eyes, that had drifted to her computer screen, flash back to my face.

"I've always wanted to write a book."

"Mmm?" I feign surprise as I sip my coffee.

She nods. "Since I was a kid."

"Why don't you do it then?"

She shrugs. "I don't really know the first thing about writing a book."

"You're a born storyteller, Darce, just open a blank document and start typing – see what comes of it."

She nibbles on her bottom lip. "I guess I could give it a go."

"I think you should do whatever makes you happiest. If that's more hours at the magazine, then do that, if it's finding hidden gems in other people's words, then do that. And if you want to write something for yourself then you know I'll support you with that too."

"Thank you," she whispers. She looks yet again, like she's going to cry.

"I won't let you struggle, princess. We're a team, I've got you and you've got me. We're in it together. I just want you to be happy, that's all that matters to me."

We stare at each other in silence for a few beats. I don't think she knows what to say, I can only hope that means I've said the right thing.

"Sometimes I hope the baby is going to be a girl, because she'd be the luckiest little girl in the world to have a daddy so sweet and considerate." I'm surprised by her train of thought, but I let her continue. "But now, just right now in this moment, I've decided that I hope it's a boy – the world needs more men like you, Ryan. You're unbelievable. If we had a son and he grew up to be half the man you are, I'd be the proudest mother on earth."

She's got *me* blushing now – a rare occurrence, but there's just something about praise from her, it means more than it does from anyone else.

"I love you, Darcy."

Her mouth falls open and she blinks at me, once, twice and then a third time.

I cross the room to stand in front of her, so I can touch her while I repeat the words I know she heard but hasn't seemed to absorb.

I take both of her hands in mine and look down into those brilliant eyes. *God,* I hope our little peanut gets those eyes. They're my favourite part of her.

"Darcy Shearer, I love you, so fucking much."

Tears pool in her eyes and she pulls me closer, burying her face against my chest. "You love me?" she asks, her unsure voice muffled against my shirt.

"Yes, I love you, princess," I say with a grin. She's so fucking sweet.

I can feel my shirt getting wet from the moisture spilling out of her eyes.

She sniffs a few times and then finally looks up at me, her eyes glassy. "I love you too, Ryan."

So much sincerity, truth and love.

Those are words I've dreamed of hearing for over eighteen hundred days.

I try to clear my throat, it feels thick, like all my emotions are stuck in there. And all of a sudden, she's not the only one with glassy eyes.

FIFTEEN

Darcy

"I'm so nervous I could puke."

"I'd really prefer if you didn't." His big, warm hand settles at the base of my spine and calms me down a little, but not nearly enough as he guides me through the doors of R&R's. "Seems like you've only just stopped the puking."

He's right, I'm on a month-long, no-vomit streak and I'd really hate to ruin it now.

Ryan and I have eaten here plenty of times over the past month or two, most of the staff know me by name now, but the one person I'm yet to encounter is Rebel. She's Ryan's best friend and not only have I never met her, but she hates me – I'm sure of it.

What I'm not sure of, is *why*.

Ryan has been assuring me all day that I'm wrong and Rebel is just a 'what you see is what you get' kind of woman. He's lying through the skin of his teeth, but I think it's kind of sweet that he's trying.

He wants the two most important women in his life – his words – to get to know each other, and after everything he's done to support me, this is the least I can do. It's the only thing he's ever asked of me. Doesn't mean I'm not scared shitless.

"You're fine, princess, it's just dinner. You had to meet her sometime. She doesn't bite."

I'm not entirely sure that's true, I'm almost one hundred percent confident that she bared her teeth at me the night I came here to tell Ryan about the baby, but I don't say that out loud. This woman is his best friend, *and* his business partner. I need her to like me if I'm going to have a shot at staying in Ryan's life, and after the past couple of months, I can't possibly imagine not staying in his life. I've fallen hard for this rough-around-the-edges, sweet, kind man, and I don't plan on giving him up for anything or anyone.

I nod as I follow his line of sight and find Rebel sitting in a booth down the back. She waves us over, and I relax a little bit. She's not shooting me a death glare. *Yet.*

"What did Steph tell you on the phone just before?" he murmurs into my ear as we cross the room.

He's trying to distract me, and even though I know exactly what he's doing, I still appreciate it.

"To put on my big-girl pants and stop being such a whiny little bitch," I reply, my mouth twitching with a grin as I recall her losing her cool with me.

He chuckles – the throaty sound doing funny things to my stomach.

My hand lands there instinctively, coming to rest on my baby bump.

His eyes follow the action, as they often do, and I can practically see the love pouring out of him. Doting is my favourite look on him. I can't wait to see him with the baby when's it's born. He's going to be the best father. If it wasn't for the fact that I've already fallen completely head over heels in love with him, I'm certain seeing him holding our child would have done the trick.

It was inevitable, falling for him. The same way I hope living happily ever after will be.

But first, I have to win over the redhead in front of me.

"You're late," she says with a raised brow as Ryan leans in to kiss her cheek, his hand never leaving my back.

"Always a pleasure to see you too, Rebel." He smirks. "This is Darcy."

"Hi," I say, my tone far shyer than I'd have preferred. I had all these grand plans of being confident and sure of myself – they went out the window the minute she locked those deep hazel, assessing eyes on me.

She's all kinds of intimidating. Tall, curvy, *beautiful*, with bright red hair and piercing eyes. I bet she has men falling at her feet daily. She's the kind of stunning you never see in real life. She's everything I'm not.

"So *you're* the famous Darcy. I was wondering if I was ever going to get to officially meet you."

I giggle nervously. "It's so good to meet you too."

Her expression doesn't change, yet I can't help but feel like she's internally screaming at me *I never said it was* good *to meet you.*

"I've heard so much about you, Ryan talks about you all the time," I ramble.

Ryan ushers me into the booth, and I couldn't be more grateful for an excuse to look away from Rebel. I need to get my shit together, and fast before she forms the impression that I'm a complete rambling idiot.

"Cute bump," Rebel remarks as I tug my dress so it sits comfortably over my expanding stomach.

"Thanks." I smile brightly before looking to Ryan and then smiling brighter. I still don't know how he does that. I've never been around someone who's made me this happy or feel this safe. "I feel like a whale."

Ryan rolls his eyes.

"When's the due date?" Rebel asks.

"September twentieth," Ryan answers before I can. "We're over halfway now."

"He or she?" She fires off another question.

Ryan stifles a laugh next to me.

I narrow my eyes at his side profile playfully. He's so smug. We had another scan – the scan where we should have been able to find out if we're having a boy or a girl, but according to Dr. Davis, our baby was playing coy and refusing to reveal their gender.

"It's a surprise," I say before he can say something smart.

Rebel nods her head, glancing back and forth between the two of us curiously as she sips her drink.

Ryan reclines back into the booth, his hand landing lazily on my thigh. I don't know how he's so at ease, I still feel like I'm about to puke, or pass out. Or both. Knowing my luck, *definitely* both.

Jimmy comes over to the table and puts a hold on any more small talk for the moment.

We order drinks and food, and then Ryan and Rebel talk about business for a while. I finally start to relax. This is the kind of conversation I can handle. No intimate questions. Nothing much more than a few nods and smiles are required on my behalf.

My mind drifts off to the baby supply shop I saw last weekend in the group of shops near Ryan's house. I wasn't sure how I was going to afford to get everything for the baby all at once, but since Ryan is still refusing to accept any type of rent from me, and seems to have an uncanny knack for locating the cash

I've stashed in various locations around the house so he can return it – I now have more money than I'm accustomed to having, so I should be able to afford the bulk of what I want.

"We all get it wrong sometimes, but you know all about that, right, Darcy?" Rebel's voice interrupts my daydream.

"Sorry, *what?*" I frown, not understanding her tone or accusation. I haven't exactly been listening, but I can't fathom what she's talking about.

"Rebel," Ryan hisses. "Don't." He shoots her a look that would kill any normal person – at least one that was capable of feeling fear – unlucky for me, his best friend seems to have balls made from brass.

"*What?*" she asks, feigning innocence. "I was just pointing out that we all make mistakes, and that Darcy, of all people, knows how that goes."

I have no idea how to respond to this. It's clear as day that Rebel is having a crack at me over something, but I have less than no idea what she's referring to. I mean, it could be the fact that I'm knocked up to my ex's twin, but that seems too obvious for such a dig.

I glance back at Ryan, hoping for some clarity, but he's still glaring at her in a way I've never seen from him before. Anger is radiating from him so intensely I swear I can almost see him shaking, and if I wasn't so nervous and confused, I think I'd find it sexy as hell.

Rebel just looks back at him, totally unfazed, one brow raised in challenge.

I feel sick and I don't even know why.

Our food arrives at that very moment, and I'm not even sure how I'm meant to eat a single bite. Filling my stomach feels like the opposite of a good idea to me right now.

We eat in awkward silence – I mostly shift food around my plate – and the minute Ryan finishes his meal, he takes my hand in his and asks me gently if I'm ready to leave. His tone is so soft and sweet, I don't know how he manages it, given that I can sense how angry he still is.

I nod, not caring that my food is barely touched. I can't wait to get the fuck out of here. I was so worried about this encounter, and somehow, it's gone even worse than I'd imagined, and I don't even know why.

He gets up without saying a word to the woman sitting opposite us, and then holds his hand out for me, to help me slip out behind him.

"This was fun, let's do it again sometime," Rebel says as he leads me away from the table without so much as a backward glance.

I follow along behind him, bewildered and intimidated.

It's not until we've been driving in the car for about ten minutes that he turns to me and finally speaks again.

"I'm so sorry, princess." His voice – the agony in it – I just want to make it better.

"It's okay."

"It's not even close to being okay," he replies quickly. "I promise you, I'll never let that happen again."

The silence stretches for a few beats.

"Why does she hate me so much?" I finally say, "she doesn't even know me, and she already can't stand me?" My voice wobbles at the end, and I feel tears welling in my eyes. "What was she talking about?"

He pulls over to the side of the road and clasps my face in his hands, forcing me to look at him.

"You've done *nothing* wrong, Darce, okay? I promise you, I'll fix this."

"She's your best friend," I carry on, almost sobbing now – stupid pregnancy hormones, "I want her to like me."

"Rebel is as stubborn as a mule, but she's wrong this time, and if she can't see that, then she has no place in our lives."

I can see the complete and utter sincerity in those green eyes of his, I know he would do it – for me... for *us*... but I also know damn well that cutting off Rebel would kill him, and it's the last thing I want.

I drag my thumb over his bottom lip, the rough scruff on his jaw grazing my skin. I don't know what to say, so I don't say anything. Instead, I kiss him.

———

"I NEED TO PEE," Steph states, as she always does, before sliding her chair out and getting up from the table.

I've been filling them in on my dinner with Rebel and what a disaster it was. I almost feel bad about saying anything now as both of my best friends have jumped straight on the bandwagon. I've unintentionally set up an 'I hate Rebel club'. That's not even what I want, or how I feel. I don't hate her, I *fear* her. She worries me, I don't know what happens if her and I can't find a way to get along. I don't know how we both fit in Ryan's life without being in each other's too.

It's a mess, one that's probably not being helped by Steph repeatedly ranting about Rebel sounding like 'a bitch' or 'a pain in the arse', and getting me all riled up, but still, I knew that's how she'd be – she's loyal to a fault and has quite the temper. I once saw her drag a chick out of a bar by her hair for saying something rude about the dress a friend of ours was wearing. Rebel and Steph would probably butt heads something chronic. At least Freya has slightly more chill and the capacity to be more diplomatic.

The ring of my cell phone startles me; I hardly ever get calls anymore. Ryan sometimes rings me on his way home from work, but he's in a meeting with his staff right now, so I'm confident it won't be him. I'm here with Steph and Freya, so it's not either of them.... Work only ever emails... there's not a lot of other options left; my circle is small.

I pull it from my bag and look at the screen, but it's a blocked number. I don't typically pick those up – my tolerance for scammers is pretty low – but it could be the doctor's office or something to do with my next check-up, so I answer.

"Hello?"

"*Darcy*," the voice on the end of the phone says, the tone familiar, but wrong. Somehow wrong.

"Ah... yes?" I reply, confused. It sounds just like Ryan, but I'm not sure. "Who's this?"

The penny drops a fraction of a second before he says the words. "This is Jacob."

My heart starts thumping against my rib cage and my palms sweat instantly.

I have no idea why Jacob would be calling me, but I know one thing – it's not going to be about anything good.

"*Jacob?*" I reply, my voice barely above a whisper. "Why are *you* calling me?"

Freya's hand lands on top of mine and I look up, wide-eyed, to meet her stare.

She doesn't even have to speak, I can tell by the expression on her face that she's worried... and pissed off.

"Can't a man call the woman he loves?"

The sound of the word 'love' coming from him makes my stomach roll. Jacob doesn't love anybody but himself. Probably never has, probably never will.

I don't know what to reply to him, I'm torn between hanging up and then smashing my phone for good measure... or ripping him to shreds for having the audacity to speak to me like he never crushed me into a million pieces. This is the man who walked out on me at the altar and never even looked back. Never gave me a reason why. Never checked to see if I was coping. He never did a thing. He just carried on with his life as though he didn't just destroy mine.

How *dare* he call me now and say something so ridiculous.

I don't know where I find the strength, or the volume, but I reply, my voice firm and sure. "What the hell do you want, Jacob?"

Steph overhears me say his name as she sits back down, her jaw dropping open when she realises I'm on the phone to the person we've been referring to as 'he who shall not be named'.

"What the fuck?" she mouths to Freya. Freya shrugs, looking more and more furious by the second. Her grip on my free hand tightens. Steph rounds the table to crouch next to me so she can press her ear to the phone and listen in.

"I want you back, Darcy. I made a mistake."

A whoosh of breath slips through my lips. What the actual fuck? I think I'm in shock.

"Is this prick for real?" Steph demands, having heard what I just heard.

In a different scenario, a different place, a different time... I would have found her outburst hilarious, but I don't even have the energy to laugh right now. I can't move. I can't speak. I can't even think straight.

Steph prises the phone from my frozen fingers and presses the end button before tossing it down onto the table with a heavy thud. I want to tell her off for being so rough, but I get it. I'd burn that thing if I could afford to replace it – it's tainted by him now.

"You didn't block his number?" Steph demands.

I look at her dumbly, unable to speak. My hand flies to my stomach, cradling it protectively. I can't explain the feeling coursing through me right now as anything other than fear. It makes no sense. Jacob has never laid a finger on me physically. He's certainly left his fair share of emotional scars, but he's never been a threat to me.

I don't know how or why, but he feels like one now.

Freya picks up my discarded phone and scrolls for a moment. "Blocked number," she explains to Steph when it becomes obvious that I'm in no way fit to contribute to this conversation.

Jacob could have called me from his own number, I haven't even blocked it. Blocking someone that wants nothing to do with you seemed kind of counterproductive, so I never bothered. But in saying that, if I'd seen his number flash across the screen, I prob-ably wouldn't have answered. I guess he knew that too.

"What did he say?" Freya asks Steph.

I'm grateful to them both for not trying to get me

to speak right now. They know me well, and they know when I need a moment inside my own head.

"He said he wants her back and that he made a mistake." Steph growls the words.

I hear Freya's sharp intake of breath. "No shit, *dickwad*, we all know you made a mistake." She mutters a string of curse words. "Who the hell does he think he is, trying to waltz back in?"

"A Steele," I reply, my voice even and dull. "He's a *Steele*."

I feel a little bad referring to their family like that, as though being a Steele is a death sentence – Ryan is a Steele too, my baby will be a Steele – but Ryan's nothing like Jacob or his father. He's not calculating, manipulative or ruthless. My baby won't be either.

"So what?" Freya scowls.

"So they always get what they want. Jacob *always* gets what he wants. I was with him for five years and I never saw him lose. Not once."

"Well not today, Satan," Steph quips, "he burnt this bridge good and proper. He'll have to get through us first."

The baby starts wriggling around, I can feel his or her little feet softly kicking me.

"I want to leave," I reply quietly.

I can't explain the feeling I'm having right now – it's like I'm too exposed here in the middle of this cafe – I feel like a sitting duck. I want to be at home – at Ryan's, in his arms where I feel safe. The only place in the world I feel like nothing can hurt me.

Ryan. I should tell Ryan about this, but I'm not sure I can, he'll completely lose the plot.

I go to stand up, but I feel all shaky.

Freya grabs my arm and loops hers through it while Steph collects up our stuff. They sort out everything, and it's not until I'm in the car, driving back to Ryan's that the tears start to fall.

SIXTEEN

Ryan

I'm running out of patience, fucking fast.

Two weeks have passed since Rebel was rude as hell to Darcy and disrespected me, and she's still yet to acknowledge that she stepped over the line.

Actually, fuck that, she didn't just step over the line – she sprinted over it, wearing one of those pairs of heels that leave permanent dents in the floorboards.

Darcy hasn't been back to R&R's with me since then, she hasn't outright said that she doesn't want to, but she's made up excuse after excuse to get out of it. We've been here for dinner a dozen times without issue, but that one time with Rebel would be enough to put anyone off.

Speak of the devil and she shall appear.

Rebel strolls into our office, her focus on her iPad as she taps away. "We need to get the dinner menu updated so I can send the proof to the printer."

I couldn't give a flying fuck about the menu. She knows what needs to be done, the fact that we're still going back and forth over it, arguing about what the final decision will be – something we *never* do – is just further fuel to the fire already smouldering away between us.

"Just add whatever you want," I mutter.

She sighs heavily. "Can you *not*? I know what will happen. I'll add it and then in a few days when we get it back from the printer, you'll bitch and moan that I didn't listen to you."

"Then add what I want and save yourself the argument later," I suggest.

I'm being a wanker, I know I am, but she's being a bitch. So I figure fair's fair.

She sets the iPad firmly on her desk and turns to glare at me. "Alright, I'm sick of this shit – let's just have it out once and for all and then we can get back to being friends because I'm tired and I do not have the patience for your moodiness today."

"That's a bit rich coming from you."

She's barking up the wrong fucking tree. If she wants a fight, she's damn well going to get one. I'm not a patient man at the best of times, and these are far from the best of times.

"Say what you want to say, Ryan, stop beating around the bush."

"It's called *tact*, and you could learn a thing or two about having some," I fire back.

She doesn't reply, just stands there, hands on her hips, her brow raised in challenge. It's infuriating.

Fine. She wants a reality check, I'll give her one.

"You were a complete bitch to Darcy the other night. You were so rude it embarrassed me."

Her expression changes, and for just a flash of a second, I see hurt before it's quickly replaced with irritation.

"Are you seriously still upset about that?"

Is she for real?

The stack of papers about our liquor license leave my hands and go flying across the room. "Yes, I'm still upset!" My voice thunders, almost making the small space shake.

She opens her mouth to respond, but I cut her off. "You disrespected not only me, but the woman I love too, and I don't know how the fuck you can justify the behaviour in that head of yours."

"It wasn't my intention."

"*Bullshit*. You knew exactly what you were doing. It's what you always do – come at people with that arrogance and attitude, acting like you're better than everyone else."

I regret it the moment I say it – it might be how she's dealt with Darcy, but it's not a fair statement about her character in general. I'm hitting below the belt.

"Tell me how you really feel," she deadpans, obvious hurt in her eyes now.

"I'm sorry."

"Don't be. Sounds like I deserve it."

"I went too far."

She drops her hands from her hips and falls into her chair. "I did too."

"I shouldn't have said that."

"I shouldn't have been such a bitch."

"No shit," I reply, the fight leaving me now that she's lost the bullshit bravado.

It's silent for a few beats between us. I know Rebel is trying to find the right words. She's not the best at admitting her fuck-ups, but I can see she's trying.

"I don't know why I was so hard on her. I guess I'm just scared that she's going to hurt you again. I've seen the way she crushed you, Ry. I don't want to see it again."

"That wasn't her fault. She's never set out to hurt me."

"I know," she replies on an exhale.

That's the first time I've ever heard her admit that out loud. For years, she's blamed Darcy. I think she just wanted someone to blame for my pain – and Darcy was where the finger got pointed when blaming my brother wasn't satisfying enough.

"I'll admit, she seems nice, but she's broken, you know that, right? I can see it in her eyes."

"Everyone is a little broken, that's life. Find me someone who says they aren't, and I'll make a liar out of them."

She nods slowly, in contemplation and agreement.

"You're dealing with a heart you didn't break, Ryan."

"Do you think I don't know that? My brother screwed her over. On the day of that wedding, she was a shell of the woman I once met, but she's back, Rebel, she's still in there, and every day I see more and more of her. We're healing each other."

She meets my eyes and I finally see acceptance in there. "*Okay.*"

"Okay, you'll stop being so hard on her?"

"I'll stop."

"Promise?"

"Want to pinky swear or can we just skip that part and go straight to the pillow fights and hair braiding?" she says with a roll of her eyes.

I smirk. She's an absolute fucking nightmare sometimes, but she always knows how to make me laugh.

"I *am* sorry," she says, her sincerity ringing true. "I know I was hard on her. I'll apologise. It was that time of the month and –"

I make a show of covering my ears. "Special time, got it."

I chuckle and duck the balled-up bit of paper she throws at me.

"You're going to be having a baby soon, a little bit of shedding of uterine walls is the least of your worries."

I grimace at her choice of words, but she's not wrong either.

"I'll talk to her when I get a chance. I know you've been avoiding this place and that's on me. I'll make it right."

"I hope you can, because she means a lot to me, and I love you, you know I do. But she wins. In any situation, any contest... she wins."

She nods in sad understanding. Rebel might not have found the right man for her yet, but she will one day, and then she'll understand where I'm coming from. I'll remind her of this when that day comes. It might make it sting a little less.

"Would you get out of here already; the meeting finished an hour ago, and I'm sure you've got better things to do tonight."

I don't need to be told twice.

I get up out of my seat. "As a matter of fact, I do."

———

I CAN'T QUITE PUT my finger on it, but I know that something isn't quite right with Darcy at the moment. She seems on edge.

She's fine when we're at home together, but it's as

though she's seeking solace in my arms for some reason. It's not that I mind; spending a couple of days in bed and on the couch, wrapped around her is my idea of a perfect time, but if something is wrong, I'd rather know – but she insists she's fine.

'Fine' – I swear to god, 'fine' is where reassurance goes to die.

I push the thought out of my mind. I'll deal with it later, right now I have to finish getting everything set up in the nursery before Darcy gets back.

I had Steph come and pick her up under the pretence of a girls' afternoon getting their nails done or some shit, when really it was all a carefully constructed ruse to get her out of the house so I could finally get all this baby crap into the house and set up.

My designer, Tia, gave me a foolproof layout that she put together a couple of weeks ago, after I got hold of Darcy's wish list from the baby store nearby. We got everything on the list and one of everything else for good measure it would seem. I'm starting to wonder if there's anything left in that store or if it's all at my house now.

I wasn't sure I was going to be able to pull this off, but with a lot of help from the store to assemble the furniture in their storage room, and a moving company that went the extra mile, it's all in here. It might not be *styled to perfection* like Tia instructed, but it's not bad for a guy with little to no home decorating skills.

I chuck the cream, knitted blanket over the side

of the cot. That wasn't on Darcy's ever-so-practical list, but it's one of the seemingly endless items that Tia added to my shopping cart without bothering to ask for my input.

She knows the drill by now. She helped me 'put together' my whole house, because according to Rebel, a couch, fridge and a TV weren't sufficient and I needed help. I still don't see the purpose of decorative cushions or little random things that do nothing, sitting on the shelves, but whatever – they add to the aesthetic apparently.

I stand back in the doorway and admire my handiwork for a moment. It's not bad – I'll give myself that. It looks like one of those nurserys you see in the baby magazines. No doubt it won't look quite so composed once there's actually a little person living in here, but for now at least, it's pretty perfect.

I can't believe that in a matter of months I'll be a father. That a baby who will eventually call me 'Dad' will be getting his or her nappy changed on that change table, and sleeping in that cot.

I know it'll be a while before the wooden blocks are being played with, or the stories are being understood, but I can't wait. I can't wait for every single second of it.

I snap a picture of the room and send it to Tia's cell.

She replies almost instantly with a 'not bad'. That's pretty high praise from her. It's quickly followed by an instruction to change the angle of the chair in the corner because it's 'making her eye twitch' but other than that, I pass with flying colours, and not a moment too soon as I hear the front door open, and Darcy and Steph's voices fill the house.

I smile as Darcy laughs at something Steph is saying. I love that sound. I could listen to it all day. I haven't heard it much lately, so rather than rushing out to meet her, I stand and listen for a while.

"Ryan?" she eventually calls out. "You here?"

"In the nursery," I call out with a grin.

She's going to shit the bed when she sees this. I just know it.

I cross the room and plant my ass in the rocking chair that's facing the door – now at the correct angle – so I'll have the perfect view of her reaction when she walks in the door.

I can hear Steph making some excuse about why she has to leave, and as much as I like Steph, I'm grateful that she's letting us have this time alone.

I hear the front door open and shut again then I listen for her quiet footsteps as she comes down the hallway towards the room.

It's the closest bedroom to mine – *ours* – and it gets the best afternoon sun, like right now as the light streams in the window.

"How was your – *woah*..."

Her eyes widen as she glances around the room, her jaw dropped open.

"Surprise." I grin.

"I... what... when..." she stutters, still looking at

everything that wasn't here when she left earlier today. "*How?*" she finally says.

"I had a little help," I admit.

She steps into the room and walks slowly towards the cot. She runs her hand gently over the soft blanket hanging on the side.

"It's the one I liked at the store."

I was hoping she'd say that. It wasn't the one on her list – this one was almost twice the price, but I remember how many times she looked at it when we walked past, so I took the risk and got it for us.

"I know. I got all the things you liked. But if there's anything that isn't right, we can take it back and get something else."

"Shut up," she surprises me by saying.

I stand and she steps towards me. "I can't believe you did all this."

She looks like she's in shock. I hope I haven't done the wrong thing by doing this without her.

I shrug. "I wanted to surprise you. I know you've been stressed lately, and I wanted to do something special."

"I'm definitely surprised," she breathes.

"Do you like it? If you don't we can – "

"It's the most beautiful room I've ever seen," she interrupts me, her eyes still travelling around the space. "I love it, I just can't believe you did all this."

Relief floods through me. She likes it.

"I did have to resort to blackmail and bribery," I

tease as I reach for her, pulling her chest against mine.

A smile graces her lips. "Who have you been blackmailing?"

"Steph – I needed her to take you out all day... and Sophie from the baby store. I had to convince her to give me the list of everything. And then my designer Tia chose everything else and planned the layout – but she charges a small fortune for her time, so if anything, I'd say *she* actually blackmailed *me*."

"You have a designer?"

"Yeah, she did the whole place for me."

Her smile grows wider. I don't understand why that pleases her so much.

I feel my brow furrow in confusion – my expression asking the question before my words get a chance.

"It's just the first time I came here... I remember thinking that the place was so well put together. It felt like a woman had been here. I was too scared to ask if you'd had a girlfriend or whatever live here before me. I'm still not sure I want to know the answer to that. I'm not sure I could have lived with myself if me turning up pregnant ruined your relationship or something."

I tuck a rogue strand of hair behind her ear and look down at her with a smile. It's not funny, but I can't help but feel amused at her worries.

As if there was anyone I'd rather have had than her.

"There's been no one but you, Darce. Other than Rebel, I haven't had a woman in this house for a long time."

She bites back a smile.

"I know it's not fair of me to like that... but I do," she admits. "I was all set to marry your brother, yet I don't like the idea of you having a life before ours got thrown together... go figure." She rolls her eyes at herself.

She's not entirely wrong, it's a little ironic and unreasonable, but I don't care. She can be as unreasonable as she likes – she's carrying my child. Little does she know that there has been no one of any significance in my life since the day I met her. I've tried to fall in love again, I really have. I've persisted where I should have given up – I've *tried*. I've met some amazing women who under different circumstances probably could have made me very happy, but I never got over Darcy. I'm not sure I ever really wanted to get over her. And now I know why.

If I'd truly moved on, if I'd managed to get over her the way I probably should have, I never would have even turned up to their wedding, let alone found my way into the bridal suite and then inside the bride.

I smirk at my crass line of thought. It's morbid and twisted, but I don't give a fuck. She's mine now, and that's all that matters.

"What are you thinking about?" she asks me curiously. It's only then that I see she's watching me –

watching my mind tick in a way that only she seems to have a knack for. It's as though she can hear my thoughts as they cross my mind.

"I was just thinking about being inside you."

Her beautiful blue eyes light up. "You're thinking about getting your dick wet, in our baby's nursery." She tsks at me.

I chuckle. "Oh, princess, it's not just in here, I think about it in all the other rooms too."

She giggles and smacks my chest lightly. "You're the worst."

"Here I was, thinking I was the *best*," I quip.

Her cheeks heat, and I can tell by her reaction that I'm bang on the money. I'm the best she's ever had and I'm more than happy about that.

She sidles closer, her arms tightening around my middle. Whatever stress I was picking up over the past few days, it's long gone now.

"So you love it?" I murmur as I lower my face towards hers.

"Almost as much as I love you," she replies against my lips.

I slant my mouth over hers, our tongues duelling, right there in the middle of our baby's room.

SEVENTEEN

Darcy

"I know about the baby."

That's all it says. A text message from a random number, about ten minutes ago.

I was on the phone to Freya, gushing over the nursery that Ryan set up for the baby and surprised me with yesterday, when the message came through.

She's already on her way over here.

It's probably not necessary, but I've been so on edge lately, jumping at shadows, freaking out every time I hear a phone ring... I know I'm going to crack soon. All this stress can't be good for the baby. I know I should have told Ryan what happened the other day, but I just couldn't. Everything between us is going so well and I didn't want to let some stupid, out-of-the-blue phone call from Jacob ruin it. I figured if I ignored it, it would just go away. I'm beginning to think I might have been wrong.

Freya shouldn't be too far away now – I wish she were already here. I'm falling apart at the seams.

I hear her car pull into the drive and a door shut with a thud, I rush to the front door and fling it open.

"Show me," she insists, holding her hand out for my phone as she comes inside, and I slam the door shut behind her.

I hand over the phone, glad to have it away from me and follow her through the house.

"What the fuck?" she mutters as she drops into a seat at the dining table.

"I don't know." I shrug. "It has to be Jacob, right?" I sink my teeth into my bottom lip. "I don't know anyone else that would send me that."

"How would he know though?"

"I don't know." I shrug.

"Would Ryan have told him?" she questions.

I shake my head quickly. I may not know what's going on here, but I know one thing, Jacob definitely did not find out about the pregnancy from his twin.

She gasps and drops the phone to the table. "He just text again."

"What does it say?" I whisper.

Her eyes widen as she picks the phone back up and reads the new message. "Is it mine?"

"That's it?"

She nods. "Guess we know for sure that it *is*

Jacob texting… and I guess anyone could have told him, it's obvious just from looking at you now."

I don't feel any relief in that knowledge, if anything, I feel worse. Jacob knows I'm pregnant and he wants to know if *my* baby is *his*.

"I hate to ask… but *could* the baby be his?" Freya questions with a grimace.

I open my mouth to say no, that's there's *no* way, but the reality is that there *is* a chance. I know it's Ryan's, not Jacob's – I just know it in my heart, but technically, there is a chance.

Jacob and I tried for a long, long time and nothing ever happened. If it were going to happen with Jake, it would have before now. I know it's not totally fool-proof, but it's certainly logical. Plus, the dates work better for Ryan and me, not for Jacob and me, but again, these things aren't foolproof – the scans have a margin of error.

"We had sex about three weeks before the wedding," I admit.

She sighs. Freya and Steph both know everything about Jacob, about us trying for a baby for such a long time, about my night with Ryan… so she knows that the likelihood of the baby being Jacob's is low – but not impossible. The odds are probably similar to those of getting pregnant from sleeping with a man once, and that's exactly what worries me.

My phone buzzes again. It interrupts my train of thought and fills me with dread in an instant.

"What is it?" I breathe.

Freya looks at me sympathetically and unlocks the screen. Her head drops forward as she reads the text. "He wants a paternity test."

My heart thumps in my chest. He wants a *paternity* test. He has no right to demand *anything* from me, but I know damn well that if he wants one, he'll get one. He'll drag me through the courts if he has to.

I can't believe this is happening.

"Maybe I should just do what he wants." My voice is so quiet and broken I almost don't recognise it.

This man, this pathetic excuse for a man... he broke my heart – hurt me more than anyone else in the world has ever hurt me, and somehow, he's still controlling me, my life, my decisions.

I can't escape him.

"I'd put money on the baby not being his, so maybe this is for the best. It'll prove the baby is Ryan's and he'll leave me alone, right?"

Freya opens her mouth to reply, but I'm still rambling.

"He can't do anything if we have a document saying that it's not his. It's a non-invasive procedure, right?"

"D, honey, *stop.*"

I look up from the table to meet Freya's concerned gaze.

"There's one slight problem."

"Of course there is, this is me we're talking about, if anything can go wrong, it will." I sigh. "What is it?"

"I don't think getting a paternity test is going to help you. Ryan and Jacob are *identical* twins; their DNA is virtually identical too..." She's using her sympathetic nurse voice – her clinic voice. The one I bet she uses to deliver crappy news to patients and families.

The penny drops.

They're identical.

"Even if the baby is Ryan's, it'll still be a match to Jacob, and vice versa. It would take a hell of a lot more than a standard paternity test to prove who of the two was the father, and in some cases, it might be impossible."

No. No, no, no, no, no.

I'm screwed. I'm carrying a baby and I can't even prove who the father is. I have a history of fucking things up, but this takes the cake. This is a new level of messed up, even for me.

"So let me get this straight." I hear my voice rise an octave as I speak. "Jacob is saying he wants a paternity test, and even if he's *not* the father, the test will come back saying that he is?"

She nods. "In a nutshell, yes. I'm so sorry, Darcy."

I don't know what she's sorry for – this is on *me*. It's entirely my own fault. I'm the one who slept with my ex-fiancés twin brother five minutes after her wedding got cancelled. I'm the one who thought it would be a good idea to try and get knocked up by the only person on the planet who shares identical DNA to the man I want nothing to do with.

I did this to myself.

"What am I going to do?" I whisper.

"Do you think he knows the baby is Ryan's?" she asks.

I don't know how he could, but I wouldn't put anything past him anymore. He's got money, resources and one hell of a habit of holding a grudge. Ryan has been a sore spot for Jacob for years; if he did know that his brother had fathered my child, it would probably only make him more determined to ruin our lives.

"I think it would be safest to assume that he knows everything." I can feel another meltdown coming on, and I don't even bother trying to talk myself down off the ledge this time. There's no easy way out here – there's only disaster. In *every* direction.

I'm having a baby and I'll never know for absolute certain who the father is.

I should have seen this coming. It couldn't be that simple. Nothing in my life ever is. I have no idea what my next move is, but I need to think, and fast.

I MANAGED to calm down enough that Freya agreed to leave me here alone. *Thank God.* Her pacing and ranting was driving me insane.

Ryan text about half an hour ago to say he'd be home in an hour or so, so I've been waiting for him so

I can tell him what's happened. I need to tell him everything so we can plan our next move together.

I know he's not going to be happy.

His hatred for his brother runs deeper than I knew.

I wasn't aware, but Freya told me that when Jacob walked out on me at the wedding, Ryan followed him and punched him so hard it broke his nose, so I can't imagine he's going to be too thrilled to hear his brother is attempting to contact me again now. Even less thrilled when he finds out that Jacob could be trying to claim *he's* the baby's father.

I've had no more texts at least, but I know Jacob, and he doesn't give up that easy. There will be more, but Ryan and I, we'll deal with it together.

There's a knock at the door and relief floods through me. He's home. Obviously forgot his key again, but he's home.

I rush to the door and fling it open without even checking to see it's him.

It's not. It's almost him, but not quite.

"Jacob." I choke out his name.

"Hello, Darcy."

His eyes rake over me, starting at my face and moving lower. I recoil in horror at the knowledge that he's seeing my protruding stomach for what I assume is the first time.

He doesn't linger at my belly though, his eyes sweeping down to my feet and back up to my eyes again.

He gives me no reaction and it's somehow more terrifying than yelling and screaming would have been.

I was right. I can tell by looking at him that he knows *everything*. He knew where to find me, which means he knows about Ryan. Nothing about this interaction is unexpected, I acknowledge.

He knows. He knows it all.

"I think you'd better let me come in."

"Ryan will be home soon," I blurt out.

He huffs out a humourless laugh. "I'm well aware of where Ryan is." It's creepy – the way he says that. Like he has eyes on Ryan, which for all I know, he does.

I don't know what to do. I should slam the door in his face and lock it behind me, but I'm scared. He'll just come back. He'll keep coming back until he's finished with whatever game he's playing.

He's a narcissist, plain and simple. It took me leaving the situation – our relationship – for me to see it, but now that I do, it's clear as day. He's cunning, manipulative, and he wants what he can't have. He's selfish and self-centred and would crush *anyone* to get ahead. It's all just collateral damage – me included.

My body moves before my brain has had time to make a decision. I step aside, and he walks inside without pausing, like he owns the place, although I very much doubt he's ever set foot inside this house. I'm quite confident he's never taken the time to visit his brother, yet looking at him, you'd think he'd come here every day for his entire life.

I used to find it endearing – the way he carried himself so confidently... now I see that's what made it so easy to listen to and believe all the things he told me – it was the complete and utter conviction he delivered his lies with.

I find him sitting in Ryan's usual spot on the couch, and I hate everything about it. I hate seeing him here. I hate that he's tainting this little piece of peace I've managed to create. I hate *him*.

I sit in the seat the farthest away from him, and even that, I do reluctantly. I want to walk out the front door and not look back – but I know that would be pointless. You can't outrun Jacob Steele.

"You look good, Darcy."

I don't reply, not only because I know I look like shit, but because I know he's not being genuine. He delivers the line like he read it directly from a script.

"I miss you. I want us to get back together."

I knew it was going to come out of his mouth, yet it still shocks me. The total absurdity of it leaves me in disbelief.

"Are you *kidding*?" I manage.

"Unfortunately not." He grinds his teeth together in irritation, and that's when I figure it out. He's not here because he wants to be – he's here because he's been ordered.

He doesn't want me any more than I want him...

which can only mean one thing. Daddy dearest snapped his fingers.

The only man out there bigger and badder than Jacob Steele is his prick of a father – Conrad Steele. He's the only person that Jacob bows down to, and I have a feeling that he's in control – this realisation only terrifies me more. That man is the devil reincarnated.

"Do I ever kid when it comes to my work?"

He doesn't, not ever, although I'm not entirely sure yet what exactly this has to do with his work.

"You walked out on me on our wedding day, you don't want me," I argue.

"I made a mistake."

Lies.

"I don't love you anymore, Jacob. I'm not sure I ever really did."

He chuckles, dark and menacing. "This isn't about *love*. Jesus Christ, Darcy, you're so naive. You live in this fairy-tale with Prince Charming and true love coming to save you. That bullshit isn't real life. Who gives a fuck about love? This is business."

And there it is. I'm not stupid, I've seen the stories, the gossip columns. I've seen the things they've said about Jacob, about the business. About how maybe he's not the best choice to be the next CEO. This story has stuck around far longer than I ever considered it would. He's the city's most eligible bachelor now, but the media still seem to want to focus on his misgivings rather than his new single life.

According to Steph, he's still being labelled as 'cunt of the year'.

He needs to clean up his appearance and the easiest way to do that, is to get me back.

"I won't do it," I say, my voice far stronger than I expected it to be.

"Oh, you'll do it alright. Unless you want to fight my name and money in court... where I'll win." He smirks knowingly. "I could make sure you never see that baby again."

A fresh wave of shock hits me. I'm obviously aware that he knows I'm pregnant, but hearing him speak about my baby makes me feel sick.

"You can't do that. This baby is nothing to do with you."

I know that I'm up shit creek without a paddle right now, but I just have to keep my cool and hope like hell that Jacob doesn't know what I do – that I'm completely and utterly fucked.

The look on his face scares me. Not because I think he's going to reach out and hurt me physically... this is worse... it's a look that says he's going to crush my soul.

"But it *is*..." he replies airily, "that's the interesting thing about identical twins. I did some research and turns out it's incredibly difficult to tell them apart by DNA... so let's say it was up for debate about who fathered that child... there would be no easy way of knowing."

Minutes of silence stretch by as I come to terms

with the reality that he's doing this on purpose. He knows as well as I do that the chances of this baby being his are next to nothing, but he doesn't care. He'll lie, manipulate and hurt anyone to get what he needs from them.

"I can't say for sure, but I think a judge would probably side with a prominent businessman over the bitter woman he left at the altar. Don't you?"

I'm screwed. So completely and totally screwed and he knows it. He knew it before he even walked in the door. This isn't about who a judge would side with, because I'd never get a fair trial. He and his father have half of the city's judges in their back pockets. This is about power, money and business.

He's got me cornered. I don't know how he's done it, but he has. He's found a way to ensure I either give him exactly what he wants, or I lose *everything*.

Even if I were to tell Ryan, even if he used every last cent he had to try and fight this, it would be nothing but a drop in the bucket up against the resources of Jacob and his father. And then not only would I have lost everything, but he will have too. We'd both have nothing.

I *can't* lose my child.

I can't let Ryan lose it all for me.

"I can reach out and break you, Darcy."

He knows. He knows he's left me with no choice. He knows everything and I, stupidly, didn't see any of it coming.

"You're a bastard." I choke out the words.

"I've been called worse."

He glances at his watch as though this interaction is keeping him from something vastly more important. As though he hasn't just destroyed my entire life in the space of ten minutes.

"It's not so bad. You can have a good life. You were happy with me once, you'll be happy again. You can buy expensive things... keep your child. Just do what you're told and don't force my hand."

"I'll never forgive you for this," I say. As though it'll change *anything*. As though he'd ever care about my forgiveness.

"I can live with that," he replies coldly.

"What am I meant to do? What do you expect me to tell Ryan?" I demand, the panic setting in thick and fast now. This all just became too real. This is going to destroy Ryan.

"I don't give a shit what you tell my good-for-nothing brother, say whatever you have to say. Do whatever you have to do."

I have to get out of here. I can't breathe.

I rush from the room, not caring that he's still here. He'll leave. He'll want to be gone before Ryan gets back – it's all part of the game.

I can't believe I thought I loved Jacob only a few months ago. I don't even know who he really is – and the parts I do know and understand, are not parts I like. I feel like a fool. I've been played.

I shut the door to the room that was set up as mine, but I haven't slept in for weeks. Ryan's room has become *our* room, but I can't face going in there right now – seeing the messy bed and knowing that I'll never get to slide back into it with his warm body wrapped around mine might break me.

This is going to crush him. He loves me. I know he does, and this baby too. I know in my heart that it's his. But I have no way to prove it. I can't prove that Jacob didn't father this child and trying will only kill us both.

I'm going to take so much from Ryan, but my choices both suck. I either break his heart and leave, he loses me and the baby, but he keeps his home, his business and his sanity. Or I stay – we fight, and in the end, all he'd be left with is me. No money, no baby. He'd hate me by the end of that. I'm no match for Jacob. I can't fight him. I won't win. No one ever does.

EIGHTEEN

Ryan

"Princess?" I call out as I close the door behind me. Normally if Darcy is home, there is music playing way too loudly and she rushes to meet me at the door, but today neither of those things greet me.

It's silent.

I don't even know for sure if she's here, it's hard to tell when she doesn't have a car parked outside. That'll make the surprise I have coming for her even sweeter.

"Darce, you home?" I call again.

That's when I see them – the two huge suitcases sitting in the hallway.

"Darcy?" My voice has an edge of panic to it now.

She emerges from her bedroom, her shoulders hunched forward, head down. I saw her only a few hours ago, yet somehow, she looks ten times frailer now than she did then.

I take a step towards her. "Darcy, what the hell is going on? Are you okay? Is the baby –"

"The baby's fine. I'm fine."

This is one of those classic female moments where saying 'I'm fine' actually means anything but. I've never seen her look more defeated or scared. Not the night she came into the bar to tell me she was pregnant, not even the night of her failed wedding. She looks like a shell of herself again – the way she did when she was with Jacob.

"What's going on?" I ask again, still desperate for some type of answer that doesn't confirm the fear coursing through my body. I know something bad is about to happen, my gut is telling me I'm about to hurt. I want so desperately to be wrong.

"I have to leave."

She can't even look at me.

"You have to leave?" I repeat, deadpan.

"We knew this was only a temporary solution, and I think now would be a good time..."

She's babbling and I tune her out.

Leave.

She's leaving me.

"*Why?*" I demand, interrupting whatever shit she's spurting. I don't understand. This makes no sense to me.

"I just think it's for the best."

"Don't lie to me. Not after everything. We don't lie to one another. If you don't want to be here then that's fine, but I don't believe that's the truth."

Her blue eyes finally meet mine and the unshed tears spill over, running in long trails down her cheeks.

"*Please*, Ryan, just let me go." She begs – *pleads* with me.

I don't understand what's going on here. We've been so happy. We *are* so happy, and now she wants out?

None of this makes any sense.

"Did something happen? If something is wrong you can talk to me, Darce, I'll help you. I'll –"

"There's nothing anyone can do," she whispers.

"What the hell does that mean?" I reach out for her, but she steps back. My hand falls into the space between us. I don't know why, but that cuts me deep – deeper than any of her words so far.

"I have to go okay; I just have to."

"*Why?* Just tell me why. I'll support you with anything, but I *need* to know why."

"I can't, okay!" she yells, the loudest I think I've ever heard her. So loud, it shocks me.

"Please don't make me say it." Her voice is a whisper now – one extreme to the other.

"Say what, Darce? I have no idea what's going on here. I'm confused as fuck."

"Then just believe me when I say I have to go. If

you really love me, you'll let me go. I have to go. I *want* to go. I don't belong here."

It's bullshit. It's all bullshit. I see through her as though she's made of glass, but I can't figure this out. I don't know why she's running from me.

"That's my baby in your belly, Darce. You're mine, both of you are."

"I'm not yours, Ryan, I never was."

It's a lie. I can see the way it tastes like poison coming from her lips, but that doesn't make it sting any less.

"You were mine from the very beginning, you just didn't know it yet."

Her brow furrows. "What is that meant to mean?"

"Nothing," I reply. "It doesn't matter, the only thing that matters is you, here with me."

A fresh wave of tears stream down her pretty pink cheeks.

"I *can't.*" I hear everything I need to hear in those two words. She's leaving. I can't change her mind. Nothing I do or say is going to stop her.

I've lost her. *Again.*

My legs feel as though they're about to give out from under me.

She must sense that I've got no fight left – nothing left to give. She wheels one of the suitcases out of the house before coming back for the other.

She returns inside once more, pausing in front of

me. I can't look at her; it'll break me. I can't watch the most important thing in my life walk out the door.

She pushes up onto her tip toes and presses a kiss to the corner of my mouth. "I'm so sorry."

That's the last thing she says before she turns and leaves, closing the front door softly behind her.

I follow her, stupidly wanting one last glance.

I watch her through the glass as she gets into a car, and behind the wheel, is none other than my brother.

My legs do give out now. I fall to the floor, a pained, guttural sound ripping up my throat.

This is the second time I've had to watch her walk away with him, and I'm not sure I'm strong enough to handle it again. It was hard enough the first time and I know damn well that was nothing compared to what this will do to me.

NINETEEN

Darcy

Jacob looked at me like I was pathetic when I told him that I wouldn't be sharing the master bedroom with him like I used to, but he didn't put up a fight as I wheeled my suitcases down the hall to one of the guest rooms.

I guess he doesn't really give a shit what happens behind closed doors. This whole thing is about public appearances after all – he likely doesn't want to share a bed with me any more than I want to share one with him. And thank God for that; the thought of laying my head next to his makes me want to jump off the balcony.

I close and lock the door behind me and flip one

of my suitcases on its side. I took one of Ryan's t-shirts, the one he was wearing yesterday. I couldn't help myself. I needed a part of him with me.

I grab it out and bring it up to my nose, inhaling deeply. This might have been a mistake. It smells like him and that makes me want to cry. I've been reduced to sniffing his clothes when only last night I had the real thing next to me.

There's a knock at my door, but I make no move to answer it.

"I'm going to work." Jacob's voice comes from the other side. That's all he says before I hear him walk away.

That's it. He doesn't care if I need anything. He doesn't care if I'm hungry or comfortable. He doesn't care about me at all.

And he never will.

I curl up in a ball on the bed as sobs begin to rack through my body. I've never hurt like this before.

Jacob leaving me at the altar was nothing compared to this. I don't need tequila to feel numb this time – I feel numb all over, as though I've been detached from reality.

I feel like my entire world has been ripped out from underneath me. Everything that made me smile... everything I loved is gone. Everything except this baby.

I rub my stomach and feel as the baby moves around inside me. "It's just me and you now, Peanut."

My voice is hoarse from all the crying, but the tears haven't stopped, they're still flowing freely down my cheeks, and I doubt they'll stop anytime soon. I have nothing worth stopping for.

My phone rings, and I roll over to see who's calling. It's Steph, but I'm not sure I can face her right now, so I let it go to voicemail.

She's probably calling to tell me about breaking one of her newly painted nails, or about how loud Mark snored last night, and I don't have the energy to care right now. I don't even have the energy to pretend to care.

The ringing stops and then starts again immediately.

I ignore that too.

A text comes through

Steph: What the fuck is going on?

Steph: I went to your house to drop off that bag you wanted.

My heart sinks.

If she went to the house, then she would have seen Ryan. I can't even imagine how he would have looked – how completely broken he would have been.

Another text comes through.

Steph: Call me now before I call the police.

I groan and hit call. Talking to anyone is the last thing I want to do, but I know Steph and I know she's not kidding. She'd have the police around here, banging the door down within the hour, and I doubt that would please Jacob.

He lectured me the entire drive over here about the perfect little wife I needed to be, the minute I set foot outside of the door. The idea makes me sick. I wonder what he'd do to me if I just flat out refused to leave the apartment. I hate being stuck inside, but it's certainly preferable to pretending I can stand the sight of him.

She picks up after only one ring. "Are you okay?" she demands.

"I'm okay," I reply through a fresh wave of tears.

"Oh, D," she says, her tone compassionate. "Talk to me. What the hell is going on?"

"I don't know where to start."

"Start with why you left the man of your dreams broken in a heap on the floor."

Pain shoots through my chest at her words. I hate that I've hurt him. I know how much this will be killing him.

This is all my fault – if I could take his pain as my own, I would, but unfortunately that's not the way the world works. People like me and Ryan... good people, we don't win. We just get ruined by the Jacobs of the world.

"I didn't have a choice," I reply.

I don't know what to tell her. Jacob didn't give me instructions on how to handle my friends. I don't know if I'm meant to tell her the nonsense public version of events, the one where we had some time apart, but couldn't cope without the other... the one where our unborn baby brought us back together... or if I'm meant to tell her the truth and swear her to secrecy.

"Darcy Shearer, I swear to God, if you don't tell me what the hell is going on right this minute, I'm going to get Mark and his friends to come over to that palace and take you out of there, and if you think security cameras and guards will stop them, you'd be wrong."

Part of me wants to let her do it – because I know damn well she isn't kidding, and much like Liam Neeson's character in *Taken*, Mark and his ex-Secret Service buddies all have a 'particular set of skills'. But I know damn well that won't last. I'm not going to go into hiding with this baby. If Jacob wanted to find me and bring me back again, he would. So, I'm stuck here.

The least I can do is be honest with my best friends. I know they won't talk – not when they know what's at stake. So that's exactly what I do. I spill everything... every last detail to Steph.

I'm bawling again by the time I'm done.

I didn't know I could cry this much.

"Oh, D..." I can't be sure, but I think she's crying too. "I could kill that cunt."

I snort a laugh. I hate that word, it's not one I

approve of, but in this particular situation I think it's fitting.

I sniff. "I don't think Mark and his friends would approve of you doing that."

I'm not actually sure that's true. I get the feeling Mark has lived through a lot of things that would keep people up at night, but the last thing I need is Steph getting any outrageous ideas. She's already obsessed with murder documentaries; I hate to think what tips she might have picked up.

"What are you going to do? He can't just leave you locked up in a gilded cage."

"He can and he will. I guess I just have to wait it out. Maybe one day when he's taken control of the business, he might let me go. I'm sure he's only doing this for his father's approval. He wants the CEO role more than anything, and Conrad is all about appearances."

"He does realise this is real life, right? This isn't some movie where you can keep women as slaves."

"I'm not sure he cares."

"You could go to the media," she suggests after a few beats.

I don't have the heart to tell her that she's not likely to come up with any lifesaving scenario that I haven't already thought of, because I've thought of them *all* and still managed to come up empty.

"He'd just take me to court," I reply.

"You know, there's nothing to say they'd side with him. You're the mother – and no one can debate that... that baby is going to be coming out of *your* hoo-hah."

"The best I could hope for is joint custody. That means leaving my baby alone with a man who I'm willing to bet doesn't actually want anything to do with him or her. I'm not doing that, Steph. Where this baby goes, I go. Even if that means being miserable for the rest of my life."

She's quiet for a long time. I can just hear her moving around quietly.

"I still say we off him," she finally says.

I laugh. It's all I can do. I'm afraid if I don't laugh, I'll cry, and God knows I've done enough of that already.

———

"JESUS, is it like this everywhere you go?" Freya demands as she glares out the window at the photographer that followed us all the way from the car to the door of the restaurant.

It's not always like this at all. Jacob and I only used to get photographed at public events or parties, but ever since I moved back into his apartment two weeks ago, I've had cameras hot on my heels every time I've walked out the door.

It's ridiculous. I know damn well that Jacob is behind this – in fact, I'd be surprised if he isn't paying these photographers out of his own pocket. At the very least, he or his minions are tipping them off.

Images of me and my noticeably expanding bump have graced the pages of four of the most popular gossip columns this past week alone.

I don't know why anyone gives a shit. I'm a nobody, and Jacob sits behind a desk all day. I bet if he were ugly, no one would care less. Unfortunately, he's far from ugly – on the outside at least – and the women of this city are eating this shit up.

Apparently, people go nuts for a 'second chance love story'.

The idea makes me want to puke. I just hope like hell that Ryan isn't seeing any of this garbage.

"Don't get me wrong, D, I like being the centre of attention, but that shit is too much, even for me." Steph flips her hair over her shoulder before sending the middle finger to the woman with the giant camera who will no doubt sit and wait for us to come back out.

"I told you we should have got food delivered to the apartment," I mumble as we slide into a booth, as far away from the front window as possible.

"We shouldn't have to," Freya argues. "Does she just wait around all day, waiting for you to do something?"

"Her or someone else. The other day I was craving bagels and when I came out onto the street there were five of them just sitting around. I went back inside. Still haven't had my bagel." I pout. It's about the only thing I've actually been excited to eat.

"You look like you haven't had *anything*. Are you gaining weight? I swear you look thinner in the face."

I shrug. "I eat when I remember. I'm not really hungry most of the time... I forget. I'm sorting it out."

I know that it's not good, but it's true. My appetite has virtually disappeared these past couple of weeks to the point where I can go an entire day without eating and not even notice.

Thankfully, I had a doctor's appointment yesterday and she knocked some much-needed sense into me. My baby can't grow without the nourishment I provide. I know this, but I've fallen so deep into this depressive hole, that I'm not sure it had really registered until I heard someone say it out loud.

I set two-hourly reminders to eat in my phone's calendar as soon as I got out of the appointment.

I have to admit, I do feel better today than I have in days.

Steph and Freya exchange a look. "I'm ordering you two of everything," Steph tells me, her tone leaving no room for argument. Not that I'd bother. I don't care anymore.

I'll eat if they tell me to eat. I'll do what they tell me I should do. It's no different with Jacob. I'm basically a trained monkey at this point.

"Did you get a dress?" Freya asks me softly, her hand landing gently on my arm.

I shake my head. "I can't find anything suitable to

fit over this bump, and I don't have enough time to get something made."

"What do you need a dress for?" Steph questions.

"Jacob wants me to go to the business awards ceremony with him."

"Have you tried that little store we went to last summer?" Freya asks at the same time that Steph says, "Tell him to shove it up his arse."

That gets a small smile out of me. My two best friends are polar opposites sometimes.

Freya ignores Steph and carries on, "I'll take you there after this, the saleswoman is the best. She always knows what looks best on someone's body type."

I nod.

I can't think of anything worse than attending this awards ceremony with Jacob, but I know I'll do it. He'll make my life hell if I don't.

I'm entirely at his mercy and he knows it.

"Darcy."

I'm pulled from my thoughts by Freya shaking my arm and saying my name for what I'm guessing isn't the first time.

"Mmm?"

"She wants to know if you'd like a drink?" She points at the waitress standing next to me, whose presence I hadn't even noticed.

I'd kill for a huge glass of wine right now, but of course, I'm in no state to be indulging. "Just water for me, thanks."

The waitress disappears again, and I see Steph and Freya exchange glances again. They're having one of those 'no words' conversations, and it doesn't take a genius to figure out what the subject is. Me. They're worried about *me*.

I don't blame them.

I'm worried about me too.

TWENTY

Ryan

There's a knock at the door. I consider just yelling out, "fuck off." But I know I shouldn't.

It's not the world's fault my life is a train wreck.

I get up from the couch, dodging the empty pizza boxes and bottles of Coke. This house is a fucking mess. *I'm* a fucking mess. I haven't showered in two days. I don't know when I last put on deodorant or ate something that wasn't predominantly made of cheese.

Whoever is on the other side of my door is in for a treat.

There's another knock as I reach it. "Yeah, yeah, I'm coming," I mutter as I swing it open.

It's just some young kid. I scowl at him. "Yeah?"

"Mr. Steele?" he questions.

"Depends on who's asking."

He shifts his weight nervously from one of his feet to the other. "I ah, I'm Kenny, I work at Automotive Plus... did no one let you know your vehicle had arrived?"

I hear blood whooshing in my ears.

Fuck.

I completely forgot about it. I haven't checked my emails all week either, so somebody probably did let me know, but I've been in no state to comprehend anything.

It's only then that I notice the brand new, shiny, black sedan parked in my driveway.

The car I bought for Darcy.

I didn't think it was possible, but I feel my heart crack open a fraction wider.

Kenny clears his throat, no doubt trying to get my attention so he can do his job and then get the fuck out of here – away from the crazy, stinky man in front of him.

I can't pull my eyes off the car.

She should be here. I should be showing her what I got for her and our baby to get around in. We should be happy, celebrating this new thing in our lives.

But we're not.

"So here are the keys," the poor bastard states.

I finally look back to him, my arm coming up robotically to take the two sets of keys he drops into my palm.

"I need you to sign here, please."

He holds out a clipboard.

I glance at his face again. I remember him now. I chewed his ear off about Darcy and the baby and everything that was going so great in my life.

The irony.

Now he probably thinks I've got them chopped in pieces in a chest freezer in the basement. I'm probably giving off some serial killer vibes right now.

I take the pen from him and scrawl my signature on the line.

"I'm meant to show you around the vehicle."

He glances behind him, and I follow his line of sight to where, who I assume is his colleague, is waiting in another vehicle.

"I won't tell if you won't," I deadpan.

He chuckles, nervous.

I feel bad for the kid. He's probably waiting for me to hit him with a chloroform-covered rag.

"Thanks," I say as he unclips my copy of the paperwork and hands it to me.

He nods, then scarpers like a cat on a hot tin roof, hightailing it across my front lawn and into the waiting car without so much as a backwards glance.

I step backwards, being careful not to let my eyes meet the vehicle that will never have the woman of my dreams behind the wheel.

I don't know what the fuck I'm going to do with it now.

I can't sell it. It's *hers*. It's in her name, and even if

it wasn't – it just wouldn't feel right to part with it. But I can't keep it here either, looking at it every day will just depress me further.

I shut the door and drop the keys and papers to the floor.

I need to take a shower. I need some sleep.

I amble down the hallway, heading for the bedroom, when I stop.

I don't know why I do it, but I stop outside the closed door of the nursery. Rebel shut the door to this room the day Darcy left me, but she may as well not have bothered. It's not as though I could forget what lies behind it. I could bleach my retinas and I'd still see this room in my mind.

I turn the handle and let the door slowly swing open.

It's exactly as we left it. *Perfect.*

I swallow deeply and cross the threshold into the room.

This is *torture.* She should be here with me. *They* should be here with me.

I shouldn't have let her leave, certainly not with him.

I should have fought. I should have done more.

I reach the cot and run my fingers over the bars. My baby was meant to sleep here one day.

The thought breaks me – sends me to my knees.

I haven't once cried. In fact, I can't recall ever crying since I was a little kid, but I'm crying now. Tears are streaming down my face and my chest feels like it has a gaping hole in the middle of it, right where my heart used to be. Because the reality is, she took that with her the day she packed up and walked out.

She took the most important part of me with her, and I know I'll never get it back. Life will go on, but I'll never recover – I'll never be the same.

I'm startled by a loud, guttural noise. It takes me a minute to realise it's come from my own mouth. Sobs are racking my body, shaking me to the core. My head feels light, like I'm spinning... I can't get enough oxygen.

"Breathe."

My eyes snap up, and I find Rebel crouching in front of me.

I haven't got the faintest idea where the hell she came from or how long she's been there, but her voice is probably one of the only ones that could reach me right now.

"Breathe," she says again.

I try to suck in more air, but it feels like I'm choking on it.

"*Easy*," she warns.

I try again, and more successfully this time.

"That's it. Nice and steady. In and out."

I don't know how long we stay there like that. Her encouraging me, her hand never leaving my shoulder.

She stays with me until my breaths are regular and my heart rate is steady.

I sigh heavily.

She rocks back and sits down on her butt next to me. "You wanna talk about it?" she asks after minutes of silence stretch on.

I don't, but I don't see how it can make it any worse at this point, so I do.

"Her car arrived today."

She nods. "It's a pretty sweet ride."

"I'm losing my mind without her, Rebel."

She doesn't say anything, just leans her head on my shoulder in a show of support.

"What are you doing here anyway?" I say after we've been quiet a while.

"I came to tell you that we won. Best new business is us, Ry, we did it."

She holds up her phone and shows me a news article, naming us as the overall winner of one of the most competitive categories. This city's most prestigious business award.

I feel something other than pain for the first time in far too long.

"I'm sorry we missed it."

I didn't attend – obviously I wasn't up to it, and Rebel refused to go without me. I feel awful now; I wish I'd had the strength.

"I'm glad we didn't go," she replies.

"Why?" I question, my voice hoarse.

"She was there, Ry, with him. I saw photos."

And just like that, the little bit of pride and joy I felt over our win is washed away.

She was there... with him.

"I want to see."

"She looks like shit."

"Show me," I demand.

"I'm not sure that's a –"

"*Show me*," I repeat.

She sighs heavily, but does as I ask, scrolling through her phone before tapping on something and then turning the screen in my direction.

It's Jacob and Darcy alright. He's wearing a suit, and Darcy is at his side, wearing a floor-length, dark blue dress that shows off her killer figure and growing bump.

Rebel was wrong, she's utterly breathtaking, but she looks thin – frail, and her eyes are holding so much pain it physically hurts my chest.

I run my finger over the screen, and Rebel leans her head on my shoulder once more. I rest my head on top of hers and we sit there, together, leaning against the empty cot, her keeping me from falling apart as I stare at the image of the woman I love with the man I hate.

———

"THAT'S IT. I can't fucking take this moping around shit anymore. We need to figure this out and it needs to be now, I'm too pretty for prison and I've contemplated offing you at least three times this morning alone." Rebel points her finger at me menacingly as she storms through the door to our shared office and slams the door shut behind her.

I've been waiting for this outburst from her, and honestly, given the absolute sack of shit I've been, I deserved it much sooner, doesn't mean I'm going to take it lying down.

It's been nearly two weeks since the day she found me at home, breaking, and I don't know that I'm any better now than I was then. I don't give a fuck about showering, I am off the couch and have expanded my diet to include Chinese takeout, but I'm not okay – I've just gotten slightly better at pretending I am.

"I thought you'd be dancing in the street," I snap back at her. "You never liked Darcy anyway, I assumed you'd be the first one lined up to say, 'I told you so'."

I'm being a prick, I know it, but she's pushing my buttons. She's been patient, so patient, but it seems today is the day that patience has finally run out. Well, she can join the fucking queue, because mine is well and truly run out too. If she's looking for a fight, she'll get one. I need to feel again – anything. And if the only way I can feel is by going to war with her, then so be it.

"I know I haven't exactly been her biggest cheerleader." Her voice is soft – not what I was expecting.

My anger all but evaporates when I see her face and the genuine worry and concern written all over it. Rebel is a lot of things, but I know she'd go to hell and back for me. She's a good friend.

I raise a brow at her.

"Okay fine, I was a total bitch to her."

"You were a bitch who'd sucked on a 'fuck you' lollipop," I amend.

"Whatever, we've already had this argument." She rolls her eyes. "That's not important right now. But look, I'm not even sure I like the chick, and even I can see that something doesn't add up here. She's in love with you, Ryan, it was as plain as day to see. I never want to see you get hurt, and I can't say I didn't have my doubts about her based on the situation, but she really does love you. I just know. I've been waiting until you had your shit together enough to see sense, but since that's not happening anytime soon, we're going to do this now. That girl loves you. Women don't just walk out on the man they love for no good reason."

I'd thought so too. Darcy looked at me with so much love in her eyes. I really thought we were going to make it.

"Obviously you're wrong."

"Doubtful." The retort is quick.

I manage a small chuckle at that. Rebel has a lot of strengths, but admitting that she might ever be wrong is not one of them.

"You said she was beside herself when she left – that it felt like she was rehearsing lines."

I nod. That's exactly what it was like. I've

relived those moments hundreds of times, and I can see now that leaving was the last thing she wanted to do. It was as though she was lying to me, but I can't figure out why she would. She left with Jacob of all people.

She shrugs, not understanding that piece of the puzzle either. "You can't just do nothing."

"If it's what she wants then it's what I have to do."

"And what about the baby? Even if Darcy has gone off the reservation, you're that kid's dad."

My words get caught in my throat as I think about even considering never meeting my child, but I choke them out anyway. "I told her there were no conditions. If she doesn't want me to be in their lives, then I have to respect that."

She ignores me. It sounds like bullshit even to my ears, so I can't exactly blame her. I know I told Darcy that, but that was *before*. Things have changed, everything is different now and there's so much more at stake.

"Exactly how big of a prick is your brother?" She's pacing the room now, classic behaviour from Rebel when she's trying to figure something out.

"Imagine the biggest prick you've ever met," I suggest.

"Doing it."

"Now go up about twenty levels and you might come close."

She stops pacing and stares at me. "I think he's

behind all of this. Maybe he's forced her to go back somehow."

I've been hurt to the point of breaking, so much so that I've barely been able to think straight, but I *have* considered that he's manipulating Darcy in some way – one of my 3am conspiracy theories. But it makes no sense. She owes him nothing. He has nothing over her. There's no reason for her to go back to him other than love or desire.

"Maybe she really does love him. Maybe I was just the closest replacement – only good enough until the real deal came back and claimed his spot."

"Oh, *fuck off*," she snaps, clearly tired of my pity party for one. "I smell a rat. Something is off and you know it."

I shrug.

She's one hundred percent right, but I'm not sure I can afford to think that way. If I try – if I do something about it and I'm wrong, and she really does love him, I'd have to relive this heartbreak all over again, and I'm not sure I'm built of strong enough shit to survive another round.

"What does your gut tell you?" Rebel asks gently.

I know what it tells me. The same thing it's told me every second since she walked out the door.

I sigh. "That she needs me."

She nods her head, one short, sharp bob, my words confirming what her instincts had already told her. "Then pick up your bottom lip and go figure out what needs to be done."

She's right. I hate that she is, but she's *so fucking* right.

I stand up, a new wave of hope flowing through me.

"And for the love of all things holy, take a shower."

I smirk at her, and it's the first real smile that's crossed my face since Darcy walked out of my life.

TWENTY-ONE

Darcy

I don't know what terrible thing I did in a former life
to deserve this, but I hate *every* second of my life.

I feel numb.

I'm having a baby   this should be the most
exciting time of my life, and all I feel is numb.

Ryan's there, I'm here, and all that's left is
nothing real.

———

"TRY ME, *JACKASS.*"

Those are the only words I clearly make out
before I hear the door to my bedroom swing open.

I know it's Steph, she's been calling me all day

and I've let every single one go to voicemail. I heard the commotion when she arrived at the apartment too. Jacob is actually home for once, and less than impressed by the presence of my friend, if the five minutes of muffled yelling between them I've just heard is anything to go by.

I barely speak to the man, and he's never actually asked me what Freya and Steph know about this situation, but I'm sure he's aware now – knowing Steph, she wouldn't have held back now that she's finally had the opportunity to speak her mind.

I've been in bed all day, watching Netflix, but not actually absorbing a single thing. This murder documentary series has been playing for hours, and I don't have the faintest idea what the main guy's name is, let alone who he supposedly killed or why.

I'm eating, but not tasting anything.

I've turned down more work from the magazine.

All in all, I'm failing at life. I can't even Netflix and chill correctly for fuck's sake.

Steph doesn't say a word as she walks in and closes the door behind her. I shift my eyes to watch her without moving my head; that seems like too much effort right now.

I can basically see the steam pouring out of her ears. I don't know what Jacob said to her, but she is *pissed*. Maybe it's not what he said, maybe it's me. I've definitely pushed her to her limits lately.

She stalks across the room, stepping over piles of clothes and shoes to get to the large, floor-length blind that's currently blocking every last bit of sunlight from entering this room.

She raises it, not giving a flying fuck about doing it slowly and letting me adjust.

I groan and throw a hand over my eyes.

"Like a fucking vampire," she grumbles to herself.

I look up, squinting against the harsh light that is now pouring in the window.

She's crouched down, collecting handfuls of clothes and washing off the floor.

I want to argue with her and tell her to leave it, I really do, but honestly, it's an absolute shit hole in here. Things might not be going well for me right now, but I'm not blind. I can see I've let this go too far.

I silently climb out of bed and waddle around, picking things up as I go and putting them away.

We work silently, side by side for about fifteen minutes.

She even takes all my dirty dishes out to the kitchen and, by the sounds of it, dumps them in the sink for someone else to deal with.

"Sit," she instructs when she re-enters the room, once again, closing the door behind her.

I do as I'm told and sit on the bed, scooting up to rest my back against the headboard.

She climbs on and sits up next to me.

"What are we going to do here, D? I can't let you live like this."

I sigh. It's the question of the century, and one

I'm not closer to finding an answer to than I was the day Jacob showed up at Ryan's house and ruined my life.

"I don't see a way out, but if you do, then by all means, tell me what it is."

"You could talk to Ryan."

I almost roll my eyes. I'm sick of hearing this from her. It's the only solution she ever comes up with. And I get it, yes, in a perfect world, I would be able to talk to Ryan and he'd swoop in and save the day. But that's not reality – that's fantasy. Jacob was right... there is no prince charming coming to save me. There's no white horse.

"Ryan can't help me. I'd only be taking him down with me. This is the best way. It's the *only* way."

"You know you're only punishing yourself, right? You have a shot at real happiness here and you're wasting it. Ryan loves you, D, he *loves* you. Not because you're pregnant, not because he wants to beat Jacob, he loves you because you're *you*. All you have to do is let him."

"It's not a matter of letting him. Jesus, Steph, do you think I don't want more? That I don't know I deserve better? I'm *miserable* here. I want more than anything to call Ryan and tell him everything. I want him to save me, but the reality is that he *can't* save me. I'd just ruin him. *Jacob* would ruin him."

"But he'd try, isn't that better than nothing?"

I know she means well, she really does, but the answer is no. It *wouldn't* be better. I don't see the point in the struggle – the loss – when the outcome is certain. There's no way around this.

"Short of fleeing the country, every scenario is a losing one."

She raises a shoulder. "You could."

"I'm not fleeing the country," I reply quickly. "No one is uprooting their entire life to save mine. It could be worse. I'm safe, warm and fed. There's a hell of a lot more injustice occurring in the world right now than what I'm dealing with."

"Oh, that's great, D, just because he's not beating you or depriving you of food, you're good, right?"

I'm so far from *good* it's laughable, but plenty of people have it much, much worse. I know that comparing myself to others doesn't help me in any way, but it's all I've got right now, and God knows I need something to hold onto.

"I need you to stop, okay? I can't keep doing this. We're going around and around in circles, and nothing is any different than when we did the last lap. I know this is a shit show. I know Ryan is miserable, but he's better off without me. We wouldn't be together if not for this baby. He never asked for any of this, and the best thing for him is to just move on with his life and forget about me."

I've never seen someone look so disappointed in me.

Steph just shakes her head at me, gets up and leaves the now clean and tidy room.

I don't call after her. I don't blame her. I deserve every ounce of her frustration.

I've hit rock bottom.

Ever since the night of that awards dinner – hearing Ryan and Rebel's name being called out, knowing that they'd been acknowledged for all their hard work, thinking for a split second that he might be there – that I might get to lay eyes on him... it was all too much for me.

Jacob's tense stance next to me, with the fake smile plastered across his face was the icing on the cake.

I folded like a piece of paper.

Even Jacob, who couldn't give a flying fuck about me, could see that I needed to get out of there, and fast.

He made up some bullshit excuse about me feeling unwell due to the pregnancy and got me out, looking every bit the doting father-to-be as he did it.

It was all a lie.

He spent the entire car ride back to his apartment on the phone, while I coached myself out of a full-blown meltdown.

I knew it was coming, but I'd just wanted to make it to the safety of my bedroom where I could do it in peace.

I've barely left the room since. That was an entire week ago.

TWENTY-TWO

Ryan

"I was right. He hired a fucking private investigator to spy on her," I hiss down the phone as I slide into the driver's seat of my car under the cover of darkness.

"What are you getting all high and mighty about, you're essentially doing the same thing," Rebel replies, full of sass. "Only difference is you're the one sneaking around in the dark and acting all stealth."

"I'm not sneaking around in the dark."

I'm *completely* sneaking around in the dark, but shit I hate it when she's right. I'm also not entirely hating this. I've always loved a mystery; I just wish that Darcy and our baby weren't in the middle of it all.

"Just tell me what you found out, some of us have a business to run. We can't all be out playing vigilante."

That makes me feel a little guilty. I've left her high and dry at R&R's lately. Firstly, because I was too much of a wreck to even get out of bed, and now, because I'm on a mission to find out what the hell my brother is up to. I'm a shitty business partner, but Rebel is taking it like a champ. She knows I would cover her arse the same way, and this is what we do – we pick up each other's slack. Secretly, I think she's just glad to see my personal hygiene standards return.

I'm finding relief in action. I'm finally doing something.

I just met with an old buddy of mine – Rusty. I still don't know what he does for a living, in fact, I don't even know his real name, but whatever his secret business is, he can find out *anything* about *anyone*. He's come in more than handy over the years, even though it tests my ethics and morals every single time.

"Rusty gave me the name of the guy that Jacob hired. This PI had eyes on Darcy for about a month before she left me. I don't know how he did it, but he had a copy of the PI's notes and the report he gave to Jacob. It's all in there, every last thing, right down to the dates she saw our doctor for ultrasounds."

"Creepy."

"Understatement."

"So he knows you knocked up his wife then?"

"She's not his fucking wife. She's not his anything," I snap.

"That's not what the gossip columns are saying."

"I don't give a shit what they're saying, get your head out of the fucking *Women's Weekly* and go and do some work, would you?"

She snorts a laugh. "What are you, eighty? No one buys magazines anymore, it's all online."

I blow out a breath. She's wrong though, I still buy them – more importantly, one. "The sentiment still stands," I say, my patience running thin. "Do you have anything genuine you want to contribute or are you just here to see how far you can get my blood pressure to rise?"

"Oh calm down," she retorts, completely unfazed by my outburst. "I'm just saying, she's *something* to him. But if I had to guess, she's a pawn – a possession. This is all about image. I'm assuming he knows that your swimmers made it to her egg."

"He knows," I confirm." And you're right... *every-thing* is about image with my father and him. His goal in life is to take over Steele Enterprises. He'd never get the green light from our old man unless everything was perfect. And I doubt that a runaway groom and a knocked-up ex is the definition of perfect."

"Your dad sounds like a real wanker."

"Only one out there worse than my brother," I reply. I don't even feel guilty for thinking of my own flesh and blood in that way anymore; I've made my peace with it. Just because you share DNA with someone, doesn't mean they have to be in your life.

It's not until that thought crosses my mind that it hits me.

We share DNA. Not only do we share it, but it's bound to be identical, because *we're* identical.

Oh my god. The pieces of the puzzle click together before my eyes.

"I know what he has over her," I say quickly, my voice shaking. "Holy fuck, it all makes sense."

"Oh god, it's bad isn't it, I bet it's bad."

"The baby's DNA..." I breathe. "It'll match mine, *and* his."

"What?" Rebel demands, confused, quickly followed by, "Ohhh. Oh my *god.* That son of a fucking bitch."

That doesn't even come close to covering it. I can't believe I didn't think of it sooner. He's black-mailing her, I know it.

"But why wouldn't she just tell you? You would have helped her."

"I don't know. Fear? I get that she'd be afraid of him. He's a powerful man. Weak where it really counts, but powerful at getting what he wants. And I'm no match for the money and standing that comes with that company. I could spend everything I have, and it still wouldn't come close. They've got judges in their pockets, friends in all the right places... and I'm just the rogue son who threw away his key to the kingdom."

"Best move you ever made, buddy."

Her words hit me right in the chest.

This is why I love Rebel; she might be a total pain in the arse, and an absolute nightmare when she wants to be, but when I really need her, she's got my back. She gets me.

"So, because you're twins, she wouldn't be able to prove that you were the father and not him, and therefore, it would become a custody battle. One that you're telling me he would win."

My blood runs cold. "That's exactly what I'm telling you."

I've seen how ruthless Jacob can be in business, it was never something that came naturally to me – I cared too much about the people working beneath me... about the companies on the other end of the business deal. But not Jacob, he cares about no one, and nothing more than he cares about Steele Industries and making it to the top. I shouldn't be surprised he's willing to stoop to this level, but I still am. This is so much bigger than business. This is Darcy's life. My life. Our child's life. I don't know how anyone could stoop so low.

Fuck. What a mess.

"What am I going to do?"

I don't expect her to actually have an answer for me, I'm not sure there is an answer to this, but a problem shared is a problem halved and all that.

"Honestly? I have no idea. But we're taking him down, one way or another."

———

FOR TWO SMART MEN, my brother and father have been incredibly stupid and careless on this particular front.

I still have access to Steele industries.

Jacob and I shared an access code when I worked for the company – our birth year – and it seems that he never thought to change it.

I haven't set foot inside that building, let alone these offices since the day I walked out of here, but I'm back now – albeit under the cover of darkness once again, and at stupid o'clock.

I have no idea what I'm hoping to find, but I have to try and find something. Jacob's life is this office, so I figure if there's anything he's hiding, it'll be here.

After hours of contemplating and scheming with Rebel, we both came to the same conclusion... If you can't beat 'em – join 'em.

Blackmail. It's the only option Jacob has left me with. I need to find some kind of dirt on him and then use it as leverage to get Darcy out of this mess.

I have no idea what I'm hoping to find, but I do know one thing, there are no shortage of dodgy dealings as far as my brother is concerned, so rather than it being a matter of 'if' I find something, it's more like 'when'. I just have to hope that I find something big enough to stop him in his tracks.

I slip through the doorway from the staircase and into the deserted reception area.

I'm confident there's no one here, but I'm still on high alert.

I also know there are no cameras on this floor. They're fakes. There's no way my father would want video evidence of some of the people that come and go from within these walls.

I pause for a moment, listening hard, then relax when I hear nothing. There are no lights on – I'm alone.

I don't want to waste any time here though, I know it's three in the morning, but Jacob is a wanker – it wouldn't surprise me if his shit-scared assistant comes in before the sun rises to get better prepared for her day of torture.

I skirt down the long hallway until I reach the door of his office. Right next to the door that once housed the desk I myself sat behind.

It's closed, but not locked. *My lucky day.*

I head straight for the huge filing cabinet that sits in the corner, but my luck is tapped out, because that *is* locked.

I move to the desk, sitting in his ridiculously huge, wanky chair while I rummage through stacks and stacks of documents and files.

It's all mundane, boring, by-the-book bullshit.

Jacob isn't stupid. I know he's unlikely to leave anything incriminating just lying around for anyone to stumble across.

I wiggle the mouse to his computer and the screen flickers to life.

It's password protected, but I looked over Jacob's shoulder hundreds of times when we worked together, and I doubt he's bothered to change it since.

I type in our mother's maiden name and grin to myself when it works like a charm.

I set to work, exploring every folder I can find. He's got several that have individual passwords, but my attempts at unlocking those fail, and I'm fairly confident those are the ones holding the good stuff.

I growl in frustration at another failed guess.

I'm wasting my time with this computer. I'm just about to log off when the banking app catches my eye. I wouldn't have a shot in hell at gaining access to the company's accounts, those codes change every few hours, and Jacob and Conrad keep the tokens on themselves at all times, but I'd be willing to bet my left nut that I could get into Jacob's personal account.

As of five years ago, he still used the same account we both had set up as teenagers. I know the number because other than the last digit, our account numbers were identical. I remember how 'cute' the lady at the bank thought she was for making matching accounts for the identical twins.

I could kiss her now though. I type in the number and guess the correct password on my third and final attempt.

I click on his chequing account and start scrolling through pages and pages of transactions.

I'm not finding anything except coffees and

expensive suits until a payment for ten thousand dollars catches my eye.

There's no reference, no name, no nothing.

I keep scrolling, looking out for anything similar, and sure enough, I find another payment for the same amount. Again, no details. But interestingly, it's exactly one month prior to the first payment I saw.

I skip back another month, and then another and another, finding the same thing over and over again.

I don't know who this payment is going to, but it's every single month for as far back as I can see. Ten thousand each time.

Ten thousand a month is nothing in the scheme of Jacob's finances, but it's still a red flag as far as I'm concerned. It's not as though he'd ever have anything to pay off... he doesn't donate to charity... he has no debt.

I scrawl a few dates down on a scrap of paper and close the app and then the computer.

I'd kill to gain access to the filing cabinet, but I know I'll never get into that fortress without the key... or causing substantial, and more importantly, noticeable damage, so I'm just going to have to accept defeat on that one.

I glance at my watch, it's just after 4am, I figure I have time to do one last check of the room before making my escape.

I head for the bookshelf. I remember when Jacob was just a kid, he'd always hide his cash inside books.

We even went as far as hollowing out the inside

of a book once. I remember our father absolutely flipping a lid when he saw us tossing out the mangled pages of one of his first edition hard backs.

I chuckle to myself at the memory. It feels like a lifetime ago that it was me and Jake against the world.

I rifle through all the books, sliding them out and shaking them by the spines to check if anything is trapped within the pages.

I've checked about a dozen books when I finally find something.

A black and gold business card with 'Elite Services' printed on one side in shiny, fancy lettering, and the name 'Candy' printed on the other side.

I roll my eyes as I turn it over in my hands a few times.

I'd be willing to bet a million dollars that this is the card for a hooker. No one who calls themselves 'Candy' is doing anything other than taking their clothes off or having sex for money.

I slide it back into the book and check the remaining few that are left on the shelf, but that's all I find.

I'm beyond frustrated. I've found nothing of any substance whatsoever.

I'm going to have to try a different approach with this. I need someone on the inside.

I slip out of Jacob's office, my mind racing as I hatch a new plan.

TWENTY-THREE

Jacob

The door closes behind me and I glance down the staircase to check I'm alone before hitting the green answer button on my cell and then the speaker icon so I can peruse the stock market while Mark chews my ear off.

"Maaacccaaa," I drawl as I answer.

"Where the fuck have you been, Steele? I've been calling."

He's been calling alright. Every fucking weekend – in his defence, it's been too long since I hit the clubs with the boys.

"Had to take care of some bullshit at home," I grunt.

"Yeah, what the hell is going on with you and Darcy? Andy said you two were back together or some shit."

"She's pregnant," I reply.

"Who? The stripper from your buck's night?" he jokes with a laugh.

I smirk. "Fuck no, bro, that's not a mistake I'd make twice. Darcy. She's knocked up. Big time."

He whistles long and low.

"How'd you manage that?"

I huff out a laugh. "*I didn't*. My good-for-nothing fucking brother did, but I've found a way to use it to my advantage."

"No fucking way! Write-off Ryan... I didn't think that fucker would have the balls."

"Neither did I, but it's worked out well for me. My old man is riding me about getting her back, and now here is she. Problem solved, and now I can finally get him out from behind that desk."

"It'll be your shout when that day comes."

I chuckle. Macca and the boys aren't like the pompous pricks I deal with every day. I lose brain cells every time I hang out with them, but it's worth it for the few hours of madness.

I hear a noise from a lower level, and I crane my neck over the railing to see who's there. All I see is an empty landing. There's no one there. I should wrap this shit up regardless; I've got far more important matters that require my attention.

"I'll talk to you later," I tell Macca. "Count me in for this Friday night."

"You fucking better show," he replies before hanging up on me.

I glance over the railing once more before exiting the stairwell and getting back to work.

TWENTY-FOUR

Ryan

I lean my back against the brick wall of the building three blocks away from Steele Industries, my breathing is so heavy, it's like I've just run a marathon rather than a few hundred metres.

I never anticipated hitting the jackpot like that. I'd been lurking around the building, waiting for Loretta to finish work. She's the only employee from the office I decided I could trust. We were close once. She cried the day I left. We were the closest things to friends as people get within that type of environment.

I was waiting on the stairs when I heard him speak. He was on the phone, and some type of guardian angel must have been watching over me, because not only did I get his end of the conversation, but I heard Mark's too.

I can't stand Mark Vanderfits; we met him in college... the guy was a complete loser and an entitled little punk back then, and judging by what I just overheard, he doesn't sound like he's done an ounce of growing up since.

But no matter how much of a complete and utter douche I think he is, I also feel like sending the guy a cheque for a hundred grand. His conversation has just given me a wildly unexpected lead.

I slide my cell out of my pocket and dial Rebel.

"Did you find her?" she demands by way of greeting.

It takes me a minute to register that she's talking about Loretta – getting her help seems so insignificant now. "No, but forget that, I got something so much better. I overheard Jacob on the phone to an old college buddy. He made some pretty incriminating comments."

"Details. *Now*," she insists.

I glance up and down the dimly lit street. I know there's no chance of Jacob seeing me here. His driver picks him up outside the building and then they drive in the opposite direction, but still... that was a narrow escape. Too close for my liking, but fuck was it worth it.

"He was telling Mark that Darcy was pregnant, and Mark made a joke about how he could have got the stripper from his buck's night pregnant."

"*Ew*," Rebel interrupts. "So, he fucked a stripper a week before he was meant to be getting married. Real classy guy, your brother."

She doesn't even know the half of it, but why anyone would ever cheat on Darcy is beyond me.

"That's not all. His response was that getting a stripper pregnant 'wouldn't be a mistake he'd make twice'."

I hear her gasp. It takes a hell of a lot to shock Rebel, but it would seem that Jacob Steele has taken the honours today.

"That seedy bastard! He got some poor bitch pregnant?"

I shrug, even though she can't see me, my eyes darting around the quiet street. I'm so jacked up, so full of adrenaline. This is it. This is exactly what I needed.

"I know my brother. There is no way he would have let some random woman have his child. He would have thrown money at her until she agreed to terminate."

"We *have* to find her, but there must be hundreds of strippers in this city."

I wait for the penny to drop, but apparently Rebel is having an off night in the world of crime fighting.

"You reckon that business card I found in his office the other night for the escort service might be a good place to start?" I drawl.

"Holy shit!" she cries. "You're wasted in hospitality; you should be a detective."

I don't know if she's being sarcastic or serious, and I also don't give a fuck. I'm onto something here. I can feel it. I didn't take the card with me, but the name 'Candy' from 'Elite Services' is burned into my brain.

"I've gotta go. I need to get the hell out of here and then get on Google and find this chick."

"You know, I was thinking of something else that you could do... and this just makes me think it'd be even more of a good idea."

"I'm listening."

"I know it's highly illegal, but you know, so is kidnapping and blackmail, so I figure it's fair game at this point."

"Continue."

"You should call Jacob's doctor's office and get them to send you out his medical records. You sound just like him... you know how to answer all his personal questions... It would be child's play."

I contemplate her suggestion. I don't know what I'd need his medical records for, but it couldn't hurt. Where Jacob is concerned, the more information the better.

"I could probably do that."

"Create a new email account that sounds legit and get them emailed over. I don't know if they'll be of any use, but if he's out there knocking up hookers and fucking strippers, he's probably sleeping with half the woman around here... maybe he'll have caught something we can have a real laugh about, if nothing else."

I chuckle. Trust Rebel to jump straight to thinking about potential STDs.

"I'll get on it," I promise her.

"Back to work, detective."

I kill the call and jump straight onto Google. I should be making a move around the block, back to my car, but I need to do this now – I'm too jumpy to wait.

If this search turns up nothing, I'll be pissed, but it won't stop me – I'd be willing to bet my life savings on the fact that Rusty could find this chick Candy if I can't, but I'd prefer to keep him out of this if it's possible.

I tap the words into the search bar and wait as a bunch of results come up on the screen.

I shake my head in disbelief at the millions of possibilities.

Turns out 'Candy' isn't exactly an exclusive name in that industry. Go figure.

I try again, this time narrowing it to within the local range and only using 'Elite Services' as a search.

I click the first link that comes up, but it doesn't look right, the branding is off. I never understood branding until I opened a business with the most 'on trend' woman in the world. It was all colour schemes, fonts, logos and layouts. And that was just the website.

Apparently, my new skills have come in handy now. The business card I found in Jacob's office was black and gold and there was a small gold crown in the corner, this site is pink and white.

Wrong.

I close it down and go to the next in the list. That one is mostly black, but with red writing.

Still wrong.

I try the next one, and my heart feels like it's caught in my throat when I see the gold crown logo.

This is it.

There's next to no information on the site, it's all very 'high end' feeling, but there is a number. I hit call and start pacing back and forth along the brick wall as it connects and then begins to ring.

"Elite Services, Monica speaking."

I freeze up, I don't know what the fuck to say here. I have no idea how old this card is, or if Candy is even still working there.

"Are you there?" Monica asks.

"Hey, yeah, I'm here, sorry."

"No need to be nervous, darlin', how can I help you today?"

Great. Now she thinks I'm nervous to book a professional to get my dick wet. *Excellent.* I pinch the bridge of my nose.

"I ah, I was just ringing to see if you had a woman named *Candy* working there... I ah..." I shake my head at myself.

"We sure do. Miss Candy is one of our finest."

My heart starts thumping heavily again. She's there. I'm so close I can almost smell it.

"Could I speak to her by any chance? Or I could leave my number with you for her to call me. It's sort of urgent..."

Monica giggles softly, if not a little forced. "Unfortunately, that's not how we do things around here. Privacy for our clients, and our girls, is of the utmost importance to us. But I can help you get all booked in for an appointment if you'd like?"

I pause my pacing of the sidewalk. Booking an appointment is absolutely *not* what I had in mind, but desperate times call for desperate measures.

"Okay."

"She's actually just had a cancellation. How does Friday at seven work for you?"

I blink once, twice, three times. "Sure."

I give her my name, get the address – about an hour's drive – and hang up.

Well fuck.

I guess I just made a booking with a hooker. This should be interesting.

———

I PULL into the car park and kill the engine. I'm a little early, but when Rebel started calling out after me to 'enjoy my hooker', I bailed from the restaurant quicker than I'd planned to.

I glance up at the sleek, black building.

I'd never have guessed that high-end hookers were behind those shiny windows, but that's the world we live in now. To be fair, I'm still not one hundred percent certain that she is a hooker. But logic would suggest.

It's been two days since I made this booking, and I still don't know what type of fucking game plan I'm going to roll with once I get in there. I'm winging it, and I'm not sure it's the best plan I've ever had.

There will be no hiding who I am, if this woman has dealt with my good-for-nothing brother, then she's going to recognise me on the spot. If she doesn't – then she's probably not the woman I'm looking for, and that scares me more than the possibility of some potentially awkward interaction.

I don't let myself think too hard about this not being the woman he was referring to. It has to be her. I *need* this before I completely lose my mind.

I glance at my watch, mumble "fuck it," and get out of the car.

I'm greeted by a very attractive woman, who leads me down a narrow hallway and into a small room with a door.

I paid my two thousand dollars upfront, with a hold on my credit card for 'extras'. I don't know what that means, and I was too shit scared to ask, but I make a mental note to ask Rebel later – that woman knows everything about everything.

"When the light turns green, you can go on in," she tells me before leaving me to sit – awkwardly as fuck – in the leather armchair outside the closed door. Everything looks and feels so plush and expensive. Whatever they're doing here, they're making good money.

The light turns green, and I jump up out of the seat. I pause at the door for a moment, taking a big, deep breath, before turning the handle and pushing it inwards.

I don't know what I was expecting – dim lighting maybe, velvet on the bed and a woman dressed in some kind of lingerie is what immediately springs to mind when I think about hookers, but I don't find any of that.

There's a bed, sure, but it's white and fresh-looking. And *Candy* is fully dressed in a pink dress.

"Hey," I say, the word coming out without any conscious thought of what might follow it.

She looks at my face, then moves her gaze down to my chest before flashing back to my face in surprise.

Her eyes widen as she stares at me.

"Jacob?" she questions. "What are you doing here?"

I swallow deeply. I guess that answers that question.

TWENTY-FIVE

Darcy

"Let's get another shot of you with your son and daughter-in-law, Mr. Steele." The event photographer ushers us together.

I find myself stuck in between Jacob and Conrad Steele, both of them have a hand gently resting on me, and it takes every last bit of my control not to gag at the unwanted contact.

There are some pretty heinous places on this earth, but right now I'd consider visiting most of them if it meant I could leave this elaborately decorated ball room.

"*Smile*, Darcy." Jacob scolds me between gritted teeth of his own fake smile. "*Miserable bitch* isn't the look we're going for."

Ever since that night at the awards ceremony – the night that Ryan and Rebel won an award, Jacob has been even more unbearable. He's completely dropped the act of playing nice for my sake. It's all about public appearances. For the most part, he entirely ignores my presence, but when he does acknowledge me at home, his tone is harsh and his words nasty. When we're out, he plays his role of 'loving fiancé' with all the skills of an Oscar-winning performer.

I can't believe I ever thought I loved this man – that I ever agreed to marry him. I was a total idiot. I was blind to his manipulation. I wanted to see the good in him, and I clung to the crumbs he fed me to keep me hooked. I was played, and I swear on the life of my unborn child, I'll never fall for his shit again. No matter how long he keeps me locked up and under his control.

I plaster a fake smile on my face, one that is likely to look more like a grimace, but it's the best I can do.

I'm no actress and being able to look happy right now would be exactly that – acting.

We 'smile' for a few more clicks of the shutter and then *finally* they let go of me.

It's a small reprieve, but at least I feel like I can breathe again without their slimy, unwanted touch on my skin.

Jacob gets called over by some business associates. He makes a show of sweeping some hair off my face and whispering in my ear, "behave yourself", before leaving me alone to go and speak with them. Having his breath at my ear makes my skin crawl.

"I know you don't understand business the way we do, but you're making a good choice here. A *smart* choice."

A choice? I'm not making a fucking *choice* at all. I'm being *forced* to do this.

Rage surges through me, but I restrain it as I turn slowly to face the tree that the apple didn't fall far from.

I don't reply as Conrad stands before me, appraising me from head to toe.

"Pregnancy suits you."

"Thank you," I murmur. I would have much rather told him to fuck off, but there are several little old ladies and their even older, considerably more powerful husbands, only a few feet away from us. Speaking my mind wouldn't serve me well right now.

"The two of you could really build an empire. Imagine the privileged life your children could lead if you'd just accept this for what it is."

Privileged life. What a complete joke. This man has obviously heavily subscribed to the view that money equals happiness.

He couldn't be more wrong.

"Child," I correct him. "Singular."

He chuckles, pausing to sip his drink before he answers me.

"Maybe just one for now, but more will follow, sweet Darcy, you mark my words."

A chill races down my spine. There is no way in hell that I'd *ever* willingly have another child with Jacob as the father. No way in hell, but that's the issue here. I'm not doing any of this willingly. I'm being forced – held at hypothetical gunpoint.

The truth is, I have no idea how far Jacob will go... what he'd do to get what he wants.

I feel bile rise up my throat and my hand instinctively flies to my mouth. I'm going to vomit – absolutely no doubt about it.

"I'm leaving," I choke out.

I rush towards the exit. I don't miss the comment about pregnancy sickness from one of the women as I flee the scene, my hand still covering my mouth in a feeble attempt to stop the vomit I know is threatening.

I make it out the front door and into the nearby, perfectly trimmed hedges before I empty the contents of my stomach.

I feel Jacob behind me, he's explaining to some concerned bystander that I'm pregnant, and his hand is resting on the small of my back, but I block him out. This display isn't for me, or for comfort, it's for prying eyes.

I can't keep doing this. I *won't*. I don't know when or how, but one of these days, I'm going to get myself out of this mess and get as far away from this man as I can.

I rub my hand across my stomach and make a promise to my baby, that this will *not* be our life.

TWENTY-SIX

Ryan

"Are you sure this is okay?" I ask for the hundredth time.

Candy – *Abbey* – is driving me back to her place so I can meet her son. *My nephew*. I still can't fucking barely believe the series of events that have unfolded within the past hour.

Once Abbey settled down and had a look at my ID, she started talking and she hasn't stopped.

She's twenty-five years old, and about three and a half years ago, Jacob got her pregnant. I didn't ask for too many details on that particular occasion, but from what I gather, she was a stripper at the time and had been hired to dance for a group of men at a buck's night – a buck's night that Jacob attended.

Apparently, she gave birth before Jacob found out about the kid, and he was less than impressed when Abbey came to him six months later, out of money, and saying he was the baby's father.

He demanded a DNA test, and when that proved he was indeed the father, he paid her off. One hundred thousand dollars upfront and ten thousand every month since.

He's been buying her silence with those payments I saw coming out of his account.

"It's more than okay, Ryan, Trent will be so excited to meet an uncle. He knows so little about his father's side of the family... unsurprising given he doesn't even know his father."

That comment makes me feel like shit, even though I know it's in no way my fault, or my burden to bear.

"He never visits you guys?"

She shakes her head but keeps her eyes on the road. "He hasn't seen Trent since he was a six-month-old baby. He'll be three this year. He sends the money, which is very generous; it's a lot of money."

I don't think there's any amount of money in the world that can make up for an absent father, but I don't say that to her. It's obvious she longs for a father-son relationship for her son, but she's accepted she'll never get it."

"Can I ask you something?"

"Of course." Her eyes dart towards me and then back front and centre.

"I don't know your situation, of course, but if Jacob is paying you regularly, why are you still working there?" I sling my thumb over my shoulder.

She sighs heavily. "Same reason I started it in the first place. I took on all my parents' debt when they died. It was fine for a while, but I had about a year off work when Trent was born, and I've never got those clients back. The hundred grand Jacob paid me went straight onto their loan, but that's not all of it. There are monthly repayments, interest... they weren't the most honest people – their situation was a lot worse than I thought. Some people actually think the house fire that killed them was an attempt at an insurance payout gone wrong. I thought it was absurd when I first heard that rumour, but now I think maybe they were onto something."

"Holy shit," I mutter.

This chick is doing it tough.

She shrugs. "It's not so bad. My brother helps out, but it's a struggle to make ends meet sometimes."

She turns down a quiet street and then into the driveway of a small, but tidy house.

"I don't mean to condone blackmail, but why didn't you just ask Jacob for more money? I'm sure you know he's got plenty of it."

She turns the key, and the engine goes quiet.

It's an old modest car, but much like the house, it appears well cared for.

"I didn't want to be that girl... you know? The one who got knocked up and then forced the dad to pay up big. I went to him when I had no other choice. He offered the other money, so I took it." She lolls her head to the side and meets my gaze. "I've been called 'white trash' all my life. Just for once, I'd like to not live up to that name. And then there's the fact that I'm terrified that if I don't stay quiet and play nice, he'll find a way to take Trent from me."

I don't think she's white trash at all. Being a stripper and an escort is certainly not the ideal lifestyle for her, but she's doing what she has to do to keep a roof over her and her son's head. I also can't blame her for the fear she has about Jacob – Darcy is living proof that he would stoop that low.

"Let's go in, he'll need to go to bed soon." She tips her head towards the house.

I feel nervous as shit as I climb out of her car. I don't know why... this isn't *my* kid. *I* haven't abandoned anyone, but I share blood with someone who has, and that's enough to have my stomach doing somersaults.

I follow her up the small path and through the front door.

The house is basic, but cosy. It feels like a home. There's a basket of toys in the corner and photos everywhere of Abbey and Trent.

I don't care what she thinks of herself, I already know she's a good mother doing her absolute best.

"Trent? I'm home!" she calls out.

There's a guy sitting on the couch in the other room who is looking at me curiously, he must be around my age – I assume this is Abbey's brother, but I don't get an introduction.

A little boy with dark blonde hair comes barrelling into the room, stopping right in front of me.

I crouch down before him, taking in every inch of his gorgeous little face before finally meeting his eyes. Bright green eyes, a perfect mirror image of mine look back at me.

Any doubts I had up until this moment, vanish. Even thoughts of making Jacob pay momentarily disappear. All I see is this little boy – my flesh and blood, and I soak in the feeling of knowing I love him already.

———

"HE WAS SO INCREDIBLE, Reb, so smart. He knows how to count to ten."

"I know." She smirks. "You told me already."

I rub my brow. "Did I? Sorry."

She smiles at me. "Don't be sorry, it's good to see you smiling again. Proud uncle looks good on you."

She's right. I feel better than I have in ages, and not only because of Trent, but because I have *hope*. I have something Jacob wants to keep hidden. I have leverage to get my family back, because that's what Darcy and the baby are; they're my family.

I can see a light at the end of the tunnel. I know I've still got a way to go, I'm running on a hunch here – assuming that Darcy still loves me, but the more sleep I get, the clearer my head becomes, and I can say now with almost one hundred percent certainty that she does. She belongs with me. The facts are all right here in front of me, I just have to finish this once and for all so they can come home where they belong.

"So, is this chick cool with you using her and the kid as blackmail for brother dearest?"

I don't particularly like it being worded that way, but that's the gist of it.

"She told me to do what I had to do."

After Trent had finally gone to bed, about an hour past his bedtime, Abbey and I had sat and talked for hours with her brother Adam.

I told them everything, every little thing from the very beginning, and when I was done, I knew I had allies for life.

Abbey trusts me not to put them in danger, but she was clear – I needed to get Darcy out of there and if that meant threatening to go to the media about her and Trent, then that's what I needed to do. She even went as far to say that she'd go to the media herself if she had to. Adam was less thrilled about that plan, but I assured them both that it wouldn't come to that.

I know Jacob, and I know he'd let hell freeze over before he let a story like that get out about himself.

"She sounds like a badass," Rebel replies, impressed.

"She is. She's young, but she's been through a lot. I admire her strength."

It isn't lost on me that she and Darcy aren't all

that different in a lot of ways, they've both lost their parents, they're both being manipulated by the same man. They've both lost control of their own lives at one point or another. I think when this whole thing is over, they could even be friends. I hope so. I fully intend for Abbey and Trent to be part of our lives.

"So, what's the plan? We go in there; all guns blazing and tell him what's up?"

I'm fucking around on my computer, so when the new email comes in, I see it right away.

"I was thinking something slightly more tactful," I murmur as I click on the notification and wait for the email to load.

It's the fake email account Rebel had me create to get hold of Jacob's medical files, which can only mean they've arrived.

I can't imagine there's anything in here that's going to be more leveraging than an illegitimate child with a professional sex worker, but it sure as shit can't hurt to look. Rebel might find something she finds entertaining.

"Tactful is boring."

I don't reply.

"Do you ever think about what might have happened if you'd just told her, if you'd been upfront with her when you first realised what had happened?"

FIVE YEARS AGO:

. . .

"SORRY I'M LATE," I call out as I rummage around in the fridge for a beer.

My mother hates it when I'm late, but I'm not exactly a big fan of the woman who gave birth to me, so I'm not all that concerned about her giving me a sour look. I'm sick to death of these bullshit family dinners she makes us do.

"We've started without you," my father replies.

I pop the top off the beer and make my way into the dining room.

I'm ready to spin a yarn about the work project I was working on that has made me late. The reality is that I'm still trying to find her.

The woman from the bar.

She's consumed me.

"The Ryman project took –" I start to say as I step into the room, my eyes scanning the table and landing on a blonde head.

My heart thumps in my chest, my blood pumping faster through my veins.

It's her.

I blink once, twice, three times, but I'm not imagining it. She's here.

"Barbie." The word leaves my lips on a whisper, but no one hears it as Jacob speaks over me.

"Ryan, this is Darcy – my girlfriend."

The world starts to spin.

I meet my brother's gaze and I can tell. He knows.

The smug bastard took her from me, and he knows exactly how much it's killing me.

OF COURSE I've thought about that. The *what if.* There's been times in my life where I've struggled to think about anything else. But that doesn't matter now. It's too late for could haves or should haves. The reality is that I didn't.

I wave Rebel over and she slides her chair around, looking over my shoulder. "Ooooooh," she coos, distracted from her prior question.

I skim past all the small talk bullshit from the nurse and open the main file attached.

Broken toe, persistent cough... dislocated thumb...

Nothing exciting over those years.

There are several STD checks, but much to Rebel's disappointment, he was clean every time.

"Lucky bastard," she grumbles.

I click onto the next page, and I swear, my heart fucking stops.

"Does that say what I think it says?" I demand, my pulse racing.

"Holy shit."

"Rebel," I snap. "Tell me that says what I think it says."

It's right there in black and white. The absolute foolproof solution to all our problems.

"It says what you think it says," she confirms, her voice shocked.

The word 'vasectomy' is printed in front of me, clear as day.

The notes read, '*vasectomy successful, specimen checked.*'

It's dated two years ago.

Two fucking years.

I held Darcy in my arms as she cried, thinking there was something wrong with *her*. It broke her fucking heart she'd been trying to get pregnant for a whole year and nothing had happened.

Now I know why.

I also now have concrete proof of what I already knew in my heart. That baby is mine. I'm the little peanut's daddy, and no one is ever going to take that from me.

I get to my feet, my desk chair skidding away from behind me.

"Where are you going?" Rebel looks up at me.

"I don't know."

I stride around the desk, to the other side of the room and back. I'm full of so much pent-up energy, I couldn't sit still right now if I tried.

"I want to go over there now and rip his fucking head off."

"I'm not going to stop you, in fact, I'll drive. Let's go."

She grabs her coat, high fives me on the way past, and we head for her car.

TWENTY-SEVEN

Darcy

I'm too fat for this crap.

I'm eight months pregnant, trying to be stealth and failing miserably. I can't hide behind *anything* without my stomach sticking a mile out. It's ridiculous.

I should just go home.

I don't know what I was hoping to achieve by coming here, but I knew it was worth a shot.

If Jacob catches me here, I can just pretend I'm picking up my game as the doting little wife, and I've come to visit my man at work.

If he doesn't catch me, well, then I don't have to make myself sick by pretending I don't hate everything about him. It's a win-win.

I slip into one of the boardrooms, and take a relaxing breath.

I can't hear a sound. It's empty, but the temporary partition wall prevents me from seeing the room, so I stay quiet, just in case. Jacob's schedule says he has a meeting in here in half an hour, so I should be able to make a safe escape from the building once he's settled in here and not potentially out roaming the halls.

I sit down to rest. This seems like as good of a spot as any to wait him out, and I shouldn't be bothered by anyone here. I used the lesser-known, back entrance to this large room; everyone else uses the door on the other side.

I lean my head back against the wall and close my eyes. I'm so tired. I'm uncomfortable and sore. Pregnancy isn't all that great after thirty weeks, but at least I'm not still spewing.

I hear the door open on the far side of the room and I freeze, listening for voices.

I can hear Lindsey, a woman who reports back to Jacob, she's droning on and on about some supplier and a bunch of other stuff I don't understand and don't care to try to.

"Tell them we want another five percent or we walk."

That's Jacob's voice.

I hear the sound of heels clicking against the hard floor and then the door opens and shuts again.

The room is quiet once more, except for the

sound of fingers tapping on a keyboard. Jacob must have come in early.

I could try and sneak out now, but given the airy silence in the room, and my newly acquired heavy footsteps, he'd likely hear me. Hell, someone a town over could hear me, I sound like an elephant.

I close my eyes again, deciding to wait him out when I hear the door open again.

I get up as quietly as I can with a belly this size and creep towards the door nearest me, waiting for some type of noise or chatter that will cover for me as I escape.

My hand is on the door handle when I hear Jacob say, "What the fuck are you doing here?"

His voice is like venom.

I pause, intrigued. He never speaks like that within these walls. I'm overwhelmed with curiosity of who he's directed it at.

"I wanted to see the look on your face when I tell you that it's over... that you lose."

My heart speeds up to a gallop. It's Ryan. *Ryan* is here.

I haven't heard his voice in far too long, but it still affects me the same way, all the way down to my toes. I know it's almost identical to Jacob's, but the two men couldn't sound more different to me now. I'd be able to tell them apart underwater.

Jacob chuckles, menacingly. "What the fuck are you going on about? I've got a meeting in half an hour, go and tell your bullshit to someone who cares."

It's Ryan's turn to laugh now and it's mocking. "I *really* don't think you'll want me to do that."

There's silence for a moment, and I take an unconscious step in the direction of the partition.

I want to hear more. I need to know why Ryan is here, speaking to a man he can't stand. I want to know what he's taunting Jacob with. Maybe I can use it to get myself out of this situation.

My brain tells me that Ryan's here for me, but I shut that thought down as quickly as it comes. I can't afford to be thinking like that. I need to keep my cool until I get more information.

"Why don't you just tell me what the fuck you're here to tell me. Some of us have work to do," Jacob sneers.

"I tracked her down, Jake." Ryan's reply makes no sense to me, but his tone is triumphant, as though he knows he's already won.

"*Who?*"

"Your baby mama."

I feel my jaw drop open. *A baby mama? Jacob has a baby?*

"I don't know what you're talking about." Jacob's arrogance is back.

"You sure about that? Because she's got a kid that looks just like us, and a pocket full of cash that she's burning through at a rapid rate of knots."

More silence. My heart is pounding like a jack-hammer inside my ribcage. *Jacob has a child.*

Tears spring to my eyes. I couldn't be more

grateful that I never got my wish of having a baby with Jacob, but still, knowing that we spent a year trying and failing, only for him to have a child with someone else, hurts – as stupid as that might be.

It's just another kick in the guts.

"I've met her, she told me everything."

More silence.

"I've met him too... he's one hell of a little boy."

A son. Jacob has a son.

"Keep your fucking nose out of my business," Jacob growls, his earlier arrogance gone and slight panic taking its place.

Ryan chuckles. "It's a bit late for that. You took something from me. You forced my hand, Jake, and now I'm gonna be calling the shots. Darcy is with *me*. End of story. You leave us alone, and I won't go to the media with the story of the city's CEO wannabe billionaire, knocking up a stripper."

A stripper?

What the actual fuck is going on here... I feel like I've been transported into an alternative dimension.

None of this makes sense. Illegitimate children and pregnant strippers... what the hell have I been blind to?

"Darcy is with me because she wants to be," Jacob retorts.

I want to scream about what bullshit that is, I want to kick and yell and make the biggest scene of all time until Ryan takes me away from here, but I need to hear the rest of this. I need to know what the fuck is going on before I make my presence known.

"Bullshit. I know everything, Jacob, I know you hired a private investigator to stalk her – *us* – I know you don't give a shit about that woman. I'm starting to think you never did."

"Is that what this is really all about?" Jacob chuckles, his laughter a mocking sound. "Are you seriously still cut up about the fact that I got her way back then instead of you?"

Ryan doesn't reply.

Jacob laughs again. "What? You think I didn't know you were in love with her? I saw that pathetic longing in your eye when you looked at her. You're like a puppy dog. Then there were the flowers you sent every year that I got credit for. Thank you for that, by the way, scored me major points, and I don't even understand what the fuck they symbolise."

I gasp. The flowers... they weren't from Jacob, they were from *Ryan*... all this time...

FOUR YEARS AGO:

I OPEN the door to the apartment and am greeted by a huge bunch of flowers.

"Miss Shearer?" the voice from behind the arrangement asks.

"That's me," I reply, confused. I never get flowers.

"Here you go." He thrusts them towards me, and I take them, struggling to hold them up.

"Who are they from?"

"There's a card on the top."

I thank him and shut the door behind me. I sit them on the bench and pull the card off. They're beautiful.

I have no idea who they're from – Jacob has never bought me flowers before – I don't know why I'm receiving them now. It's not my birthday, it's not our anniversary yet.

I slip the soft pink card out of the envelope and read the words written in scrawled handwriting.

"I couldn't send you the moon, but here are all of the stars."

I flip it over and find a note from the florist about the flowers. I hear my sharp intake of breath when I read that these are starflowers.

He remembered.

I grab my phone and check the date. It's been exactly one year since the day I met Jacob – the day I told him about my parents saying 'to the moon and all of the stars'.

I can't believe he remembered.

I smile to myself. Jacob might be closed off and hard to read at times, but things like this prove to me that he's a good man, that he's the man for me.

. . .

I CAN'T BELIEVE it was Ryan. Year after year. But I still don't understand. *Why* would Ryan be sending me flowers? I didn't meet Ryan until I'd been dating Jacob for a few weeks. None of this makes any sense. I have so many questions and, right now, I can't ask any of them.

"Why'd you do it?" Ryan demands. "We're brothers, and you *screwed* me."

"I saw something I wanted. I saw an opportunity and I reached out and took it. It's not my fault you were too chicken shit to do anything about it."

I creep to the edge of the partition wall and peer around it.

They're standing toe to toe, both of their chests heaving. They're both so angry. I've never seen Ryan look so terrifying.

"She's mine," Ryan growls. "Has been since that night in the bar."

That night in the bar... Ryan was there?

"I don't give a fuck," Jacob spits. "She left with *me*. She always chooses *me*. You mess with me, Ryan, and I'll fuck you both. I can take that kid she's growing, and you know it."

Ryan's chin lifts in defiance. I don't know what it is about him right now, but his stance, his energy tells me that he's got this.

"I think you'd have a pretty hard time proving that you fathered her baby, when your swimmers don't even work... don't you think?"

They're on the other side of the room, but I can see Jacob's face pale from here.

The silence stretches between them.

"Yeah... I know about the vasectomy you had done two years ago. You're a real piece of shit, you know that?"

A vasectomy.

Jacob had a *vasectomy*. *Two* years ago. That fucking prick. All that time I spent peeing on sticks... all those moments of disappointment.

"You and I both know that baby is mine, Jake, and it wouldn't take more than five minutes to prove it. I don't care how many judges you bribe, you can't argue with science."

Game, set, match.

I was right. Ryan has him right where he wants him.

"You know what, I was starting to think you didn't have any Steele in you, but I see that ruthlessness now." Jacob almost sounds impressed.

"I'm *nothing* like you," Ryan sneers. "This isn't about money or power. It's about the woman I love and the child who I want to grow up as far away as possible from men like you."

"*Everything* is about power," Jacob argues.

"I guess that's where we're different. Game over, Jake, you lose. You might have taken her from me then, but you're not taking her from me now."

It all happens so fast. Jacob lunges for Ryan, but he's too quick, anticipating his move and shifting his weight so Jacob misses. Ryan swings, connecting with Jacob's jaw before Jacob retaliates and lands a punch to Ryan's mid-section.

I don't know where I find the strength, it must be the adrenaline kicking in, because I stride forward, towards the two of them.

"Stop!" I scream.

Punches keep flying.

"I SAID FUCKING STOP!"

They freeze, and ironically, the identical twins turn their heads towards me in a perfectly synchronized motion.

TWENTY-EIGHT

Ryan

"Darce?" I breathe. I blink a couple of times, just to make sure I'm not seeing things.

"What are you doing here?" Jacob demands.

I want to punch him again, just purely for the use of that tone with her, but my woman already looks like she's seen a ghost, so I won't. Not for now at least.

"What the fuck is going on?" Her voice shakes.

She stops a few metres away, eyeing us both cautiously. I don't know what she's doing here or how much she's heard, but it's irrelevant. The only thing that matters is that she's right here. In front of my eyes. She's here and she's okay.

I feel like I breathe easy for the first time in

months, but it's short-lived as I really look at her. She looks stressed and exhausted.

She rests her hands on her lower back, the discomfort clear on her face.

Her bump has grown so much in the past couple of months. She hasn't got long to go now until the baby comes. *Our* baby.

I take a step towards her, but she holds up her hand in a motion that stops me.

"Just stay where you are. I want answers from both of you and I want them *now*."

There's no arguing with that tone, even if I wanted to – which I don't. I'm tired of keeping things from her. No more secrets.

I freeze. Even Jacob doesn't move.

I've got that prick's nuts in a vice and he knows it, but I can't help but feel like mine are right in there with his. Darcy looks anything but impressed with the pair of us.

"You have a child?" She narrows her eyes at Jacob.

He doesn't answer, just lifts his chin arrogantly.

I smack him in the ribs, hard. "Answer her."

He grunts in pain but nods his head.

"How old?"

"Three," Jacob replies, unsure.

"*Nearly* three," I correct him.

I see the tears well in her eyes. Not only did he have a child that she knew nothing about, but he conceived that child during their relationship. He's a fucking tool of the worst kind. I can't even imagine how much this information would hurt her.

I'm about to lay into him again when I see the change in Darcy. She blinks the tears away and straightens her spine.

"You had a vasectomy after that?" she asks, all the emotion gone from her voice.

"I did."

She nods, silent for a few beats before looking him dead in the eye. "*Fuck you*, Jacob."

Fuck, she's the strongest woman I've ever met. I want to give her a round of applause.

The coward doesn't even reply. He doesn't apologise. He doesn't do anything. He just stands there.

He basically kidnapped her – he's been holding her hostage for weeks and weeks, and I can tell he feels not one ounce of remorse for it. It might not be going to pay off for him in the long run, but he'd do it all over again, given the same situation – he'd do *anything* to get himself ahead.

"I'm leaving, and if I *ever* see you again, I'm going to the media – with everything, do you understand me?" she threatens him.

"It wasn't personal, Darcy, for fuck's sake," he snaps.

"*Really?*" she yells, her voice going from zero to one hundred in a flash. "It wasn't *personal?* Felt pretty fucking personal when I cried over not being able to get pregnant. It feels pretty *personal* that I gave you *everything* and you still went out cheating on me. And it sure as hell felt personal when you've held me and my unborn child against my will."

Fuck, I want to pull her into my arms and hold her so tight that all that hurt and anger just melts away, but that's not what she wants from me in this moment, and I won't take anything from her, I'm not my brother.

"Get out," she snaps at him.

"This is my fucking boardroom," he says in disbelief.

She glares at him. "I can stay right here and keep yelling if you prefer? Maybe I'll open the door. I know how much the PAs love a good bit of gossip."

He wants to stay and argue – I can tell he's dying to try and manipulate her into doing what he wants, but he's also not stupid, he knows he's beat.

He mutters a string of profanities under his breath before grabbing his laptop and storming from the room.

I don't know how he's going to explain his dishevelled appearance to his colleagues, but it'd be entertaining to hear him try. He's got a ripped shirt and a bleeding lip – not a great look for such a 'powerful' and 'in control' man.

I watch the door shut behind him and turn slowly back to face Darcy.

She looks terrible, like she hasn't slept in weeks,

but she's still stunning. I've never felt such relief just from laying eyes on a person.

"You okay, princess?"

"No." She shakes her head. "I'm *so* far from okay."

I take a timid step in her direction. "I'm *so* sorry."

"I can't believe this. You have a nephew?"

I nod, a smile crossing my lips. Trent is the only good thing to come out of this mess. "*We* have a nephew. He's amazing, Darce, you're going to love him. Our little peanut has a cousin."

Her expression softens and a smile lifts the corner of her mouth. I know part of her longs for a big family with kids running around together.

I take another step toward her.

"Stop," she whispers. "I have questions. I need to know what the hell just happened, without you close. I can't think straight when you're close."

As satisfying as that comment might be, I still feel fear. She's clearly overheard mine and Jacob's entire conversation, which means she knows I've kept something from her. She's a smart woman, it won't take much for her to figure it out. I want her to know, but I'm shit scared of the consequences.

"You were there the night I met Jacob? The dress up night... you were there?" She frowns.

I nod. "I was."

"I need to know what you two were talking about. How did Jacob take me from you, Ryan?"

Fuck, this isn't how I wanted to do this. I wanted to tell her under different circumstances. She looks so tired, so stressed, and I'm sure this is only going to add to it, but I've got no choice now. All I can do is be honest with her and hope she understands.

"It wasn't Jacob you met at the bar. It was *me*."

Her hand flies up to cover her mouth, her beautiful big eyes widening as the words hang in the air between us.

"How? What?" she whispers.

"We thought it would be funny to dress up together. One of us was meant to be Clark Kent and the other one Superman. But Jacob didn't listen, and we both turned up as Superman. Identical twins... identical costumes... I'm sure you can put the pieces together."

"*Oh my god.*"

"We talked for what felt like hours, do you remember that?"

"*Of course* I remember," she breathes. "I spent years chasing the connection I felt with Jacob on that first night."

My heart is beating so fast she can probably hear it. "You never found it?"

"Not until the night of the wedding when you came to the hotel room. It was *you* I needed. That's why there was always something missing with him."

I'm elated and terrified in the same moment. These are words I've longed to hear, but I'm scared shitless about how she's going to handle this dropped bomb.

"Do you remember I went to the bathroom right after we nearly kissed… and when I came back, you were gone. I spent weeks trying to find out who you were. Then I turned up to family dinner that Sunday, and boom. There you were. With *him*."

"I asked him about that first night, you know. He didn't remember anything much. Said he was too drunk. I filled in the blanks for him. How stupid am I?"

I shake my head. "He remembered. He knew what he was doing when he took you from me. And you're not stupid. How could you have known?"

Her eyes fill with tears again. "Why didn't you tell me?" Her tone is pained, the betrayal she feels is right there, front and centre. It hits me square in the chest, like she's swung a sledgehammer at me.

"I wanted to, Darce, but what was I meant to do? You were so happy. He was happy. I didn't want to be the one that ruined that. I just wanted to see you smile, and that night at dinner… the way you looked at him… all you did was smile."

She goes to reply, but I'm not done.

"So I pulled away. I made changes in my life – I chased my passions. I became my own man, and I convinced myself that this way, when I met someone who made me feel the way you did, I'd never be mistaken for Jacob again."

"*Ryan*," she whispers, my words hurting her. "It would have been different if I'd known."

"But it doesn't matter. None of it matters anymore. Not where I go, what I do, or who I meet... I can never find what I'm looking for because there's only one you, Darcy. I just want you."

"Imagine how different your life might be if you'd just told me five years ago that it was you!"

"That's the thing, princess, that's the *only* thing I'm thankful for in this whole mess. That man was *never* me. *This* is me, the real me. I'm living a life I love and that's because of you. I love my life now – all that's missing from it is *you*."

"You didn't like your life before?"

I shake my head. "I feel like my life only truly started when I met you. Meeting you made me the man I am today."

This is all too much for her, I can see how overwhelmed she is; her head is practically spinning.

"I want to hold you so bad."

I want her in my arms more than words can describe, but I won't make a move unless she tells me it's okay.

She covers her face with her hands and groans. "This is why Rebel hates me, isn't it? Because I was too dumb to see something so obvious. She can't stand me because I hurt you all these years."

All the pieces are clicking together for her.

"She doesn't hate you."

"She hates me."

"I really don't think this is the most pressing matter right now."

Her eyes flash up to meet mine. "No, you're right. That would probably be the fact that the man I was meant to marry is a cheating bastard with a secret child, or the fact that the man I'm completely head over heels in love with has kept a secret from me for years on end."

I swallow deeply, my throat thick.

"I'm so sorry, Darcy. I know I should have told you."

"*Of course* you should have told me. If not five years ago, then at the very least, on the night of my wedding."

"You were already going through so much... you couldn't handle any more." I know it's not entirely true. Sure, it was part of it, but I know how strong this woman is. She could have handled it. I was being selfish.

"That's not for you to decide," she replies, her voice rising an octave. She takes a step backwards, and I can physically feel the change in distance.

"*Darcy.*" It's a plea. *Don't do this.*

"I don't know what to say to you right now. There's so many lies. I need some time. I need some space."

I suck in a breath, my lungs failing to get enough oxygen.

She can't leave.

I don't want her to leave.

But as I watch her turn and slowly walk from the room, I know I need to respect her wishes, no matter how much it kills me. It's lucky for me that Rebel dropped me off, I can barely see straight, let alone drive safely. But unluckily for her, she's about to get called to come and pick up the pieces, yet again.

TWENTY-NINE

Darcy

"Holy. Fucking. Shit."

"I know." I sigh.

"Holyfuckingshit." She repeats it so quickly that the words run into one another.

"*I know*." I roll my eyes.

I know it's a shock, I get it. *Obviously*, but I'm getting a little bit over the dramatic reaction from Steph. She's done nothing but curse and make ridiculous facials for the past twenty minutes.

"You know, if I knew all you could offer was to drop a bunch of f-bombs and give absolutely no constructive advice, I wouldn't have bothered making you come home from work."

"Oh, take a day off, this is *insane*, I need to process. This is my process."

I can't help but laugh at her, however exasperating it might be for me. She's not entirely wrong. I did just dump a hell of a lot on both her and Freya, but still. I need them to give me something helpful.

Freya has barely said a word, she's just been sitting next to me, holding my hand in silent support. I actually don't know what's worse, her complete lack of reaction, or Steph's over-the-top one.

I called a taxi from the Steele Industries offices, went straight back to Jacob's apartment, packed my shit and left – for good. I even left the taxi running outside so it could take me straight to Freya's and out of that five-star hell hole.

The look of relief on Freya's face when I knocked on the door, bag in hand, is something I'll never forget.

I knew I'd been worrying my best friends, and rightfully so, but it probably hadn't sunk in just how concerned they really were for me. I can't even imagine watching either of them go through something like this, knowing there's nothing I could do to help.

"I can't believe he has a kid." That's Freya. *Finally*.

"I know," I whisper. "I got the impression he has nothing to do with him. He didn't even know how old he was... What kind of man can know he has a son out there and want nothing to do with him?"

"A prick like Jacob," Steph replies, flopping down next to me and casually laying a hand on my belly. "You're huge, by the way."

I shake my head in amusement. "Gee thanks."

She rolls her eyes dramatically. "You know what I mean. I'd put my money on this kid popping out early. There's no way you're going to last another four weeks."

I've been thinking the same thing. The size of my bump, my level of discomfort and the twinges I've been feeling in my back these past few days all indicate that I'm likely to go into labour early, but I'm hardly an expert on the matter, so I could be completely wrong.

"I guess we'll just have to wait and see," I murmur.

The thought of going into labour and having this baby without Ryan by my side makes me feel like my throat is closing up, but I can't be around him right now. Not until I figure this all out.

"What did Ryan say when you left?"

I nibble on my bottom lip as I think about it. The expression on his face has been doing a loop through my brain ever since I turned and walked away from him. He looked *broken*, but he respected me enough to allow me to do what I needed to do.

That's the difference between Ryan and Jacob – one of the many differences at that.

Well, that's what I thought to be true. Now I'm not so sure. My whole life feels like a lie.

"Nothing," I reply. "He just let me go."

"Huh," Steph muses. "Can I just point out a silver lining here for a second?"

"Shoot."

"At least you know with one hundred percent certainty that your kid's dad isn't that absolute prick... like don't get me wrong, he's a total knob for getting his balls snipped and not telling you, but the world doesn't need any more Jacob Steeles, ya know? It's a real positive."

"Preach," I reply.

"I'm sure the stripper and the secret kid would have been enough bargaining power to get him to leave you alone, but you always would have wondered which one was the father of your baby. I'm glad you don't have that worry."

I'm glad too. The idea that Jacob fathered this child, as unlikely as that might be, still kept me awake at night far too many times. She's right. I probably would have always wondered.

"You know what you should do?"

"Dare I ask?" I mutter.

"You should blackmail Jake for millions and then disappear to Mexico and get yourself a boy toy."

A giggle slips through my lips.

"For fuck's sake, Steph, don't make me knock some sense into you." Freya shakes her head in disbelief.

Steph erupts into laughter. "Oh *please*, you couldn't hit water if you fell out of a boat."

"That's a lie and you know it. I've been taking those combat classes at the gym."

"Yeah, for two whole weeks. I'm shaking over here," Steph teases.

I feel tears welling in my eyes.

"Now look what you've done," Freya scolds Steph as a drop of moisture rolls down my cheek.

I shake my head. "They're happy tears. I've missed this. I've missed you both so much."

Freya gives me a small smile, the banter with Steph forgotten, and rests her head on my shoulder. Steph does the same on the other side, and finally I feel some of the stress leave my tense body.

These girls are such a rock-solid support fixture in my life, I don't know how I got so lucky.

We sit there like that for a long time. Them comforting, me thinking. All of us, together.

"You love him," Freya says after a long period of silence in which my tears have run dry.

I don't have to ask who's she's talking about; we all know it's Ryan, not Jacob. It was never about Jacob. It hasn't been about Jacob for a long time now.

Sure, I'm hurt by his actions, he betrayed me back then when he should have been loyal, but he doesn't have any bearing on my life anymore. I'm free of him. He can't hurt me because there's nothing left there – I don't love him anymore.

My heart is held by a completely different man.

Looking at the two of them side by side today, I can't believe I ever mistook one for the other. They're so different. Ryan's eyes, his expression, his energy is soft and warm... Jacob's is harsh and indifferent. Ryan looks at the world with wonder – Jacob looks at it with critical eyes. They might have been born identical, but they're virtually strangers now.

"I love him," I confirm.

And apparently, he's loved me for years.

"You need to let him in, D. He loves you. He never meant to hurt you."

I know this. I know he never set out to cause me pain, but the unfortunate reality is that he has. I know he must have been hurting himself, seeing me with Jacob after the night we shared, but he could have said something. He *should* have said something.

That night... that was something else. I've *never* felt a connection so instant, so intense, that quickly. He felt like home within a space of minutes.

FIVE YEARS AGO:

HE'S STANDING SO close to me, my head is spinning – it could be the drinks, but I doubt it. I've been drunk more times than I can count, and it's never felt like this.

He lowers his head a fraction, gauging my reaction to his proximity.

I tilt my chin up towards him, welcoming him closer.

I've been waiting all night for him to kiss me.

We've talked and talked – about everything and nothing, it's so effortless with him, it seems too good to be true.

God, I want him to kiss me.

His lip curves up at the corner as though he can read the thoughts going through my head and is amused by them.

He's so handsome... that kind of gorgeous you only see on social media through a heavy filter. But there's no filter here.

"You alright, Barbie?" he murmurs as he winds his hand around the back of my neck and into my hair.

I nod.

My breath hitches as he bumps his nose against mine.

He smells like whiskey and deliciousness.

He's so close, I can feel the warmth of his breath on my face, but he's not close enough, not yet.

His tongue darts out to moisten his lips and my belly flips.

He leans in... and someone yelling "wooooo! Beer pong!" crashes into us.

I hear him chuckle as he steadies me. The moment is lost, but I can't be too mad about it. I know damn well we'll get another one – I'm not going to let this one get away.

"I need the bathroom," he tells me, his eyes looking over every inch of my face before meeting my gaze. "Wait right here, okay?"

"Where would I possibly go?" I tease.

He runs his thumb down my cheek, gives me one last, longing look and then heads for the bathroom.

LESS THAN FIVE minutes later he was taking my hand and dragging me out the door behind him.

Only now I know it wasn't him at all. It was Jacob.

————

"NOT THAT I don't appreciate the fact that you're eating again, but you haven't done anything *but* eat in two days, D. I think it might be time to put down the ice cream and go get your man."

She's right, I know she's right. I miss Ryan like crazy and knowing that I'm free to see him whenever I want, but we're still not together, is driving me mad, but the reality is that I'm scared. Terrified even.

Every time I open my heart to someone, I get hurt, and that scares me.

"I know. I'm being a baby."

She reaches out and takes the tub of ice cream from my hands. I scowl at her but give it up. She's right, I've made up for two months of barely eating by stuffing my face for two days straight. I feel sick.

"You're not a baby, you're afraid, and that's fair enough. You're allowed to be pissed, you can yell at him, cry... do whatever you want... but just do *some-*

thing, please, for the love of God, do something other than sit on my couch like a sack of shit."

I giggle at her exasperated tone. "Tell me how you really feel."

She huffs out a laugh. "Look, I love you, D, but you and I both know you're not going to let this ruin what you have with him, so just get on with it. You're having a baby together... Ryan will be going stir crazy without you. Put the poor man out of his misery."

I hate the thought of him hurt or upset. I also hate the thought of my life without him.

We belong together, I know we do. We just need to sort out these minor details and we'll make it. I know we can make it.

"Okay." I nod. "I'll go and talk to him.

"Finally, she sees the light." She reaches up to the sky dramatically. "Let's go, I'll drive you myself before you can change your mind."

I flip her off and then extend my hand to her to help me off the couch. I'm not about to turn down a ride.

My belly tightens uncomfortably as she gently helps me up – I rub at it until the feeling eases.

I can feel my not-so-little peanut squirming around. "Not much room left in there, huh, baby," I muse.

I go and check my reflection in the mirror, making sure my outfit looks alright, even though there's only so much you can wear when you're the size of a house, but I want to look as good as I can when I see Ryan again.

I start waddling towards the door – because that's the only realistic way to describe my walk these days – when another wave of pain hits me.

"Urgh." I groan. "Man, this kid is giving me a hard time today."

Freya eyes me sceptically. "Are you okay?"

I realise I'm almost doubled over. I slowly straighten as the tension fades. "I'm alright. Let's go."

I only make it into the basement, to the side of Freya's car before it happens again.

Freya glances at her watch. "Ah, so... I don't mean to alarm you... but I think you might be in labour."

"No way, it's just a bit of discomfort," I argue.

"It's *a lot* of discomfort, every five minutes. Now, I might not be a midwife, but I am a nurse, and I'm telling you, you're in labour."

"Shit," I mutter. "I'm four weeks early." My voice trembles.

I've been waiting for this baby to come, I've been fully prepared to meet him or her early, but now that it might actually be happening, I'm terrified. Four weeks is a long time in terms of baby growing. I also don't have my shit together at all. I'm not ready.

Her expression softens. "It's okay. Let's just get you to the hospital and they'll check everything for you okay."

"What about Ryan?"

Suddenly I don't care about all the revelations of

the past week. I just want Ryan. I want to feel like I'm safe.

"I'll call him from the car," she reassures me as she opens my door and tries to usher me in. I don't move, I'm starting to panic.

"I don't even have a baby bag."

She looks at me sympathetically.

"We don't know that the baby is coming yet, but we do need to get you checked out. Let's just get there. One step at a time. I can get anything the baby needs if and when."

"Okay." I nod. I take a step towards the open door before pausing again.

"I don't have my birth plan."

She tries to refrain from rolling her eyes but fails spectacularly. "It's exiting your body one way or another, what happens between now and then is nothing you can plan for, *trust* me."

I nod again, wide-eyed. "Okay." I still don't move.

"I love you, D, but *get* in the car. If I have to call Ryan and tell him that you've given birth to a premature baby in a basement carpark because I couldn't get you to hop in the goddamn car, he's going to *kill* me."

"Okay," I repeat, like a skipping record, but this time when she helps me into the seat, I let her.

I'm strapped in and we're heading down the block in the direction of the hospital before the next, what I now assume to be a contraction, hits.

"Oh man." I groan. "They're getting worse."

"I'm calling Ryan," she says as she hits the phone button on her steering wheel.

"Hey, Freya." Ryan's voice fills the car after only a few short rings.

"Ryan, hey, so listen, Darcy seems to be having contractions, we're on our way to the hospital but she doesn't have anything with her, and I don't know who your doctor is."

"She's in labour?" His voice sounds robotic. "Right now?"

I watch the colour return to my knuckles as I release the death grip I had on the handle of the car. My breath comes in heavy pants.

Steph glances at me before looking back at the road.

"Sure seems that way," she confirms. "She's just had another contraction, she's pretty uncomfortable."

That seems to spur him into action. "Why didn't you call me?!"

Steph sighs. "I'm calling you right now, and I really need you to keep your cool, for Darcy."

"Sorry, sorry," he mutters. "I just... is she okay?"

"I'm fine," I answer him. And I am, I'm one hundred times calmer just for hearing his voice.

"*Darcy*," he breathes. "I'm coming, okay, princess? I'll be there soon with everything for you and the baby, and I'll call Dr. Davis on my way."

"Thank you," I whisper, my emotions on overload.

"I love you, Darce. You and that baby are my

whole world, and I'm so sorry if you've ever felt otherwise."

"I love you too," I reply softly.

"You guys are *so* cute," Freya gushes. "But we've got to go, we're just pulling into the carpark."

"I'll be there in fifteen minutes," he promises before the call ends.

Fifteen minutes.

I can manage fifteen minutes, and then Ryan will be here, and we can figure the rest out together. I just have to get through the next fifteen minutes.

Freya parks the car and kills the engine before looking at me. "You ready?"

I take a deep breath, then nod. I doubt anyone is ever really ready, but I'm as ready as I'll ever be.

THIRTY

Ryan

No amount of planning can make you ready for this.

Seeing the woman you love, in absolute agony as she tries to navigate getting your child out of her body, is not something that any pregnancy or birthing book can prepare you for.

I arrived with two minutes to spare on my fifteen-minute deadline, and I've never seen Darcy look so scared. Her eyes found mine and she reached out for me immediately. Any fear I had of her shutting me out, evaporated in that moment. She needed me as much as I needed her.

We need each other right now.

Dr. Davis – *Courtney* – arrived about a half-hour

ago, near twenty minutes after I did, and thank fuck for that. I've never felt so completely and utterly helpless in my entire life.

"You're doing great, Darcy, that's it, just breathe through it," Courtney – who Darcy still refuses to call by her first name – encourages.

It's just the three of us in the room now, although I'm confident Steph would be right here next to me if Freya hadn't have insisted they give us privacy.

It only took Courtney about five minutes and a quick examination to confirm that Darcy was in fact in established labour, and that our baby was on its way.

I'm terrified it's too soon – that the baby shouldn't be coming this early, but Courtney is the picture of relaxation. She keeps reassuring us both that plenty of babies are born completely happy and healthy at thirty-six weeks and that ours will likely be no different.

I won't be satisfied with that until I see with my own eyes, but right now I have more important things to worry about.

Darcy grips my hand so tight I'm worried it'll have lost all function forever by the time she's done, but I don't say shit about it. I'm not stupid enough for that. She's in the most intense pain a person can experience, and I'm just along for the ride – crushed fingers and all.

"You okay, princess?" I ask softly as I wipe her forehead with a damp cloth.

She nods, her eyes sagging closed with exhaustion. She's so tired. She's strong, but she's running out of steam, and I don't blame her, just watching her go through this has left me feeling drained. It feels like it's been hours.

"I'm just going to examine you again, Darcy, see how many centimetres we're at."

Darcy nods without opening her eyes as Courtney lifts the hospital gown and feels around under there.

I like to think of myself as a pretty strong man, but I have gone nowhere near the far end of that bed. A buddy of mine warned me that it wasn't for the faint-hearted, and I'm not sure I've got the stomach for whatever the hell is going to occur before too much longer.

"This is great, Darcy, really great, you're dilated to ten centimetres now, I think we might have to manually break your waters and see if we can get things really going and get you pushing."

I don't know what the fuck manually breaking someone's waters involves, it doesn't sound pleasant, but I smile at Darcy, gently squeeze her hand and hope like hell that she can't read the blind fear in my eyes. "You okay with that, princess?"

"*Anything* to get this baby out of me." She groans.

I watch with wide eyes as Courtney calls in two of the nurses, they exchange words before one of them hands her a knitting-needle-looking thing with a hook on the end. My eyes widen further as I realise she's about to shove said thing up my woman.

What happens next is a blur. There are pads and towels being handed in and out and a puddle of something wet on the floor by my foot. Darcy moans – loudly – and I hear Courtney telling her to breathe and then push on the contraction.

I do the same, repeating 'breathe' and 'push' like some kind of expert, rather than an unprepared moron who has no idea what he's doing.

Ten pushes is all it takes, and then I hear it. The cry of a baby. The cry of *our* baby.

It's a sound I'm sure I'm going to dread hearing over the coming weeks, months, years... but right now, it is music to my ears.

I kiss her damp forehead, covered in matted hair. "You did it, Darce."

I know I'm crying, but I don't care. I'm so over-whelmed. I can't believe how strong Darcy is. This woman is seriously incredible.

Courtney holds up a tiny, pink, wrinkly little baby. "Congratulations, it's a healthy little boy."

I look at him, his wrinkly skin, his tiny fingers and toes, his wide, screaming mouth. He's *perfect*.

"It's a boy," Darcy whispers, her voice thick. "I hope he's going to be just like you."

I cry even harder.

————

"LIAM?" I suggest.

She shakes her head, her eyes never leaving the tiny bundle in my arms.

Our boy weighed in at six pounds on the dot and in perfect health. I made sure. Twice.

We've had him for a few hours now, and Darcy desperately wants to name him tonight, so I'm dredging up every boy's name I can think of and hoping like hell that one of them appeals to her soon. She desperately needs some sleep.

"Scott?"

She just frowns.

"Adam? Aiden? Bronson? Brett? Carter? Daniel? Ethan? Evan?" I fire off in quick succession, fully prepared to make my way through the entire alphabet if that's what it takes.

"Wait." She stops me, holding up a finger.

I pause, hopeful that I've said something she likes the sound of. At this point I don't care what she chooses, she's done all the hard work – she deserves the honour of making the choice. I just want her to finally rest.

"Carter," she says softly. "I think I like Carter."

I tread carefully, not wanting to spook her by coming on too strong.

I sit down gently on the edge of her bed so she can see our little boy's sleeping face.

"Does he look like a Carter?" I ask, even though I've never understood that concept. He just looks like a squishy baby to me.

She nibbles on her bottom lip and leans forward to look right at him, her cheek resting on my shoulder.

"I think so."

"I like it," I tell her. I do really like it, but I'd probably agree to her calling him Shrek at this point.

"Carter Steele." She tests it out. "Sounds right to me."

I feel like I'm about to fucking cry all over again. I wasn't sure she'd want him to have my last name. I've been such a little bitch today – I've never cried so much in my life.

"You want him to be a Steele?"

She smiles, her gaze leaving our son and meeting mine. "Of course I do. You're a Steele, and so is he."

She'll be a Steele too someday.

"Carter Steele." I nod. "That's the winner. Our son has his name."

"He's so cute, Ryan. Holy shit we make a good-looking baby."

"That's all you, princess. I could look at him all night, but I need you to sleep. Okay? I've got him, and I'll wake you if he needs anything."

"I'm scared to shut my eyes. What if I wake up and none of this is real?"

She's so fucking sweet. I kiss the top of her head. "I promise you, it's real. It's the most real thing in the world and we'll be right here in that chair, watching you sleep."

She yawns and lies back into the pillows. "You promise?"

"Swear on my life, Darce. Just rest."

She nods sleepily, her eyes already drifting shut.

She's out to it within minutes.

I move gingerly off the bed, careful not to wake her, and take up residence in the big armchair next to the bed.

Carter doesn't even stir as I get comfortable.

I sit there with him, marvelling at his perfection for almost two hours, during which time a nurse comes in and instructs me what time Darcy needs to feed him. I negotiate an extra hour of sleep for them both, turning on the best of my charm for the blushing nurse. That hour flies by too and before I know it, it's time to wake her. And I have just the thing.

I carefully set Carter down in the small bassinet that he's yet to lie in and turn to find the bag I packed for the hospital.

This has been right under Darcy's nose this whole time and she's had no idea.

I slip the small velvet box from the hidden, inner pocket where I stashed it months ago and flick open the lid, sliding the over-the-top diamond ring out from within the fold.

I glance at Carter again, but he's still out to it. "Let's surprise your mumma," I whisper.

I carefully pick up her left hand and slide the ring onto her ring finger. I'm adjusting it when I feel her pull on her hand and then gasp when she sees what I've done.

"What are you doing?" she whispers.

I don't know if she's trying not to wake the baby, or if I've shocked her into almost silence.

"I know we have things to talk about, and I know I have apologies to make, but I also know that I don't want to spend another day not knowing if you'll be my wife one day, Darcy."

She brings her other hand up to her face to cover her mouth in surprise as I hold her other hand hostage in mine.

"Darcy Shearer, I want forever with you. Nothing is right without you by my side. I love you. I love you so fucking much. Will you marry me?"

"Don't swear in front of the baby," she whispers, her eyes welling with tears.

"Sorry." I chuckle.

She holds my eyes for a moment before shifting her focus to the ring already on her finger, and then finally back to me again.

"Yes." She nods, the tears spilling over. "Yes, I'll marry you."

She throws herself into my arms and I hold her tight.

"I'm so sorry," I start to tell her, but she shushes me.

"It doesn't matter right now. I understand why you didn't tell me, and we've got nothing but time to figure this out. We'll be fine, Ryan. We'll be *incredible*."

"I love you so much."

"To the moon and all of the stars," she replies, her voice thick with emotion.

"To the moon and all of the stars."

EPILOGUE

Ryan

It's not quite the peaceful homecoming I imagined, but it's perfect in our own, chaotic way.

The house is bustling with noise and females. The two things seem to go hand in hand it turns out.

"You better get used to being outnumbered, buddy. It's just you and me versus all these girls." I speak softly to my son as I bounce him gently in my arms.

My son.

I still can't get used to that. I have a son. And he's beautiful. Every last inch of him is the most incredible thing I've ever seen.

He looks just like me, but I think he's going to

have his mum's eyes. They're getting lighter by the day. I hope he does. They're the most amazing eyes.

I can hear Rebel telling Freya some outrageous story in the kitchen, and Steph is chiming in with equally as outrageous suggestions on the matter.

"You're never going to be short on crazy aunties giving out even crazier advice, that's for damn sure," I tell him with a smirk.

He pouts his lips in his sleep, his brow furrowing before his face smooths out again and he drifts back into a deeper slumber.

I could watch this kid sleep forever and I don't think the novelty would ever really wear off. I'm smitten as hell with this little boy.

"Why are you two hiding out here?" Darcy whispers from the doorway.

She's leaning against the frame, watching us. I have no idea how long she's been there, listening to me talk to our little boy.

"THERE'S TOO many girls out there, isn't that right, little man?"

He responds by continuing to sleep.

"We're severely outnumbered. I could feel my testosterone levels slipping."

Darcy huffs out a laugh. "Mark is here."

"Mark is whipped. He's no better than having another girl in the house these days."

Darcy rolls her eyes. "He is *not* whipped. He's a trained killer. He's *doting*."

I raise a brow at her. "I get that Steph is pregnant and all, but she is going to rip the absolute piss with that man, mark my words. Next time we see her, she'll be sipping a virgin cocktail, being fanned by an oversized leaf while he wishes he'd escaped to an island off the coast of Mexico while he still had the chance."

Darcy giggles. "You're an arse."

I smirk at her. "Maybe, but I'm still not wrong."

Steph spilled the beans on being knocked up the minute she laid eyes on Carter for the first time. I've never seen anything like it, it was as though she took being 'clucky' to the next level and just had to get it out. Mark wasn't even mad that she told everyone the news early.

He is *so* whipped.

"Who the hell is hogging the baby?" Rebel's voice comes from behind Darcy, before she too, appears in the doorway.

"Give that kid to his Godmother already," she demands, stretching her arms towards me. "You've had him all day."

We asked Rebel to be his Godmother not long after he was born. He doesn't have a Godfather, instead the poor kid has another two Godmothers. None of us are even religious, but I was told it was a 'thing' by the woman I plan to spend the rest of my life with, and quite frankly, after watching what Darcy went through to give birth to our son, I'd have agreed to pretty much anything she wanted – three Godmothers included.

"How about you come back and have a turn at about three in the morning when he's screaming his head off," I offer.

"Firm no," she retorts with a glare. "Now hand him over."

"I'd give him up, biker boy, she'll scratch your eyes out," Darcy says with a giggle.

Rebel and Darcy meet eyes and exchange a look that is full of knowing, understanding and amusement.

I never thought I'd see the day, but it's here – they're friends – *really* friends. I don't know what went on between the two of them when Rebel visited us in the hospital nearly a week ago, but when I left them alone, things were tense and awkward, and by the time I returned, they were laughing like old friends.

Whatever was said between the two of them, I'm grateful for it. Nothing makes me happier than seeing all the people I love and care about most, all under one roof.

I walk towards Rebel and carefully, if not a little awkwardly, hand Carter over. I've had sweet fuck all experience with babies, so this has been a massive learning curve for me. Not Darcy though, she's an absolute natural.

I don't know how she does it, but she's totally in

tune with him and his needs. I could change his nappy, feed him, and hug him to try and settle him, but she'll be the one who knows instantly that he's crying because he has wind.

She amazes me more and more with every passing hour of our new lives.

"You take him in there for a bit, I want to show Darcy something," I tell Rebel as I grab Darcy's hand.

"Where are we going?" she quizzes me as I lead her down the hallway towards our bedroom.

"I didn't have time to get you a real push present... especially after the car situation," I admit sheepishly, "but I did get you this."

Darcy nearly killed me when she found out I'd bought her a brand-new car. She loves it, but she was adamant it was far too much. Silly woman still doesn't realise that nothing is ever too much when it comes to her.

I turn her by the shoulders and point at the framed picture on the wall of our bedroom.

"Oh my god, it's *not*." She laughs.

I chuckle. "Sure is, princess, our one-way ticket to hell, right here in the flesh."

She crosses the space and runs a finger over the glass housing our signed agreement, on the ripped-out page of the bible.

"I can't believe you kept that."

"I can't believe you said we were going to hell," I tease.

"I can't believe we broke *every* one of those rules."

I turn her to face me and wrap her up in my arms. "I had my fingers crossed the entire time."

"Dirty rotten cheat." She giggles.

"I would do anything if it meant keeping you, Darcy Shearer."

"You're lucky I already agreed to forever then, right?" she says, my ring glistening on her finger.

Lucky doesn't even cover it.

There aren't words. I could arrange every letter of the alphabet into every possible combination of words and phrases, and I still wouldn't find the right words, but I'll settle for being called lucky.

The luckiest man in the world.

misspelled. They are slang terms and form part of everyday, New Zealand vernacular.

I.e: I'm from New Zealand and sometimes we say weird things down here... please try and be cool about it.

Thanks again!

ALSO BY

Love like Yours Series

Rushed – Book 1

Pierced – Book 2

Hunted – Book 3

Chased – Book 4

Love like Yours Box Set – Books 1-4

Rock Games Novels

Paper, Scissors, Rock: Vol. 1

Hide and Seek: Vol. 2

My Heart Duet

My Heart Needs

My Heart Wants

Every Last Beat – The Heart Duet Box Set – Books 1 & 2

Calendar Boys

Mr. January

Mr. February

Mr. March

Mr. April

Mr. May

Mr. June

Mr. July

Mr. August

Mr. September

Mr. October

Mr. November

Mr. December

Calendar Boys Box Set – Books 1-4

Calendar Boys Box Set – Books 5-8

Calendar Boys Box Set – Books 9-12

ACKNOWLEDGMENTS

It's been a long time coming, but I'm finally back in the swing of things and putting out a book that I love, I hope you all enjoyed reading it!

Shout out to my friends and family – all the special people in my life, for encouraging (nagging) me to get this done, it's finally here, you can all leave me alone now!

Special thanks to my girls, Bianca, Stacey and MV, for always having my back, helping me bounce ideas and listening to my moaning. I wouldn't want to do this gig without you all, and I appreciate your support, always!

Thank you so much to Stacey and Trina at spellbound for the excellent job on editing, as per usual!

Last but definitely not least, thank you to my readers, new and old, for picking up this book and making it all the way to the end, you're the best!

Nicole x

PLAYLIST

Fix a Heart – Demi Lovato
Sunday Morning – Mitch James
Chose You – Stan Walker
You should be sad – Halsey
I Found You – Andy Grammer
The Good Ones – Gabby Barrett
I Am Yours – Andy Grammer
July – Noah Cyrus
Favorite Part Of Me – Astrid S
You & Me – James TW
Rise Up – Andra Day
Fast Car – Taio Cruz
Still Falling For You – Ellie Goulding
The Bones – Maren Morris & Hozier
Like This – Jake Scott
Keep Holding On – Avril Lavigne
I Choose You – Ryann Darling
Never Seen Anything "Quite Like You" – The Script

I Could Get Used To This – Becky Hill & WEISS
I'm Ready – Sam Smith & Demi Lovato
Times Like These – Live Lounge Allstars
Passport Home – JP Cooper
Feel Good – Gryffin, ILLENIUM & Daya
Back To You – Selena Gomez
Should've Been Me – Naughty Boy, Kyla & Popcaan
False Alarm – Matoma & Becky Hill
I Can't Make You Love Me – Teddy Swims
Selfish – Future & Rihanna
No One Compares To You – Jack & Jack
World of Our Own – Westlife
Run to You – Lea Michelle
No Judgement – Niall Horan
Wonder – Shawn Mendes
Falling Like The Stars – James Arthur
All I Want – Kodaline
Wherever You Are – Kodaline
Dancing On My Own – Calum Scott
Next To You – Chris Brown & Justin Bieber
Next To Me – Imagine Dragons
Marry Me – Jason Derulo
Holding You – Ginny Blackmore & Stan Walker
Say You Won't Let Go – James Arthur
Unwritten – Natasha Beddingfield
Meant to Be – Bebe Rexha & Florida Georgia Line
Fallin' – Jessica Mauboy
Who Knew – P!nk
Don't Hold Your Breath – Nicole Scherzinger
Come See About Me – Nicki Minaj

WITHOUT YOU – The Kid LAROI & Miley
Cyrus
Space For Two – Mr. Probz
All These Years – Camila Cabello
Teenager in Love – Madison Beer
In Case You Didn't Know – Boyce Avenue
Unsteady – X Ambassadors
Take Care – Drake & Rihanna
enough for you – Olivia Rodrigo
Remember – Becky Hill & David Guetta

ABOUT THE AUTHOR

NICOLE S. GOODIN is a romance author and mother of two from Taranaki in the North Island of New Zealand.

In mid-2015, she started to write about a group of characters who wouldn't get out of her head. Her first book, Rushed, was published in mid-2016.

Nicole enjoys long walks on the beach, pillow fights and braiding her friends' hair. She dislikes clichés, talking about herself in the third person, and people who don't understand her sense of humour.

Please feel free to contact her either via her website, email, Instagram, Twitter or on her Facebook page, she would love to hear your feedback. If you're feeling really game, you can even sign up for her newsletter.

UPCOMING TITLES

Rock Games Novels

One for the money